The White Marble Burzi and Other Stories

Sharat Kumar

THE WHITE MARBLE BURZI AND OTHER STORIES
Sharat Kumar

First Published 2017

ISBN 978-93-83723-18-8

Published by
LG PUBLISHERS DISTRIBUTORS
49, Street No. 14, Pratap Nagar,
Mayur Vihar Phase I, Delhi 110091
Email: lgpdist@gmail.com

Designed by
Limited Colors, Delhi 110 092

Printed at
Sapra Brothers, Delhi 110 092

We Love because it is the only true adventure

Nikki Giovanni

Fiction is like a spider's web, attached ever so lightly perhaps, but still attached to life at all Four corners.
Often the attachment is scarcely perceptible

Virginia Woolf

Contents

Acknowledgement

My grateful thanks to Jehanara Wasi who encouraged me to publish this collection of short stories after discussing the idea with me. She also provided meticulous support of her remarkable linguistic and editorial skills to hone the manuscript at all stages of production.

I would also like to thank Anjali Capila firstly for putting me in touch with Jehanara Wasi. And secondly, for always being the first person to read the stories and offer her invaluable suggestions.

My sincere thanks also to Mr. K.K. Saxena for not only agreeing to publish this book, but also for his flexible attitude to gracefully accept all changes proposed by me even at advanced stages of production.

Sharat Kumar

Preface

George Bernard Shaw reportedly said that his real interest lay in the prefaces since he could freely use them to expound his social ideas, and he wrote his plays only because they enabled him to publish the prefaces. Lacking such vision, I can only say that the idea of writing a preface came to me as a consequence of writing some of the stories included in this volume, which attempt to explore the elusive mystery of human relationships with their unending complexities.

A question was raised in the course of a talk delivered by me when I said that of the three principal areas of human life—physical body, intellect, and emotions—it is 'emotions' which exercise paramount influence on the quality of a person's life. The question was that since it is the intellectual ability which has brought unprecedented physical comforts to human life, it is the intellect, and not emotions, which should be considered of primary value.

In response, I suggested imagining a situation where a person dear to us has died. We get so distraught that we can neither sleep nor eat. Our 'intellect' then points out that these actions cannot bring the dead person back to life. We accept this 'intellectually', yet we still cannot eat or sleep. And, if our 'intellect' is really sharp, it will tell us 'don't you know that in a few weeks time you will be sleeping, eating, and even laughing, quite easily'? While we also accept the truth of this, we still cannot eat and sleep.

Most of our formal education aims at sharpening the intellect. It has little to do with the emotional aspects of life. Emotional development remains a matter of experiences we undergo, starting from childhood or even earlier when we are still in the womb. Long before rational faculties develop in a child, his inner self (unconscious mind or *antaratma*) has already absorbed several experiences from his surroundings. Most important of these are perhaps from the quality of life his parents' lead, which play a major role in the decision-making processes in his life. Modifying these in later years is only possible with a determined conscious effort, which is not an easy process.

In the normal course of life, we have little awareness of the mental activities churning inside us. The characters of a work of fiction, however, take us through the thought processes of many minds, and ultimately of our own mind. Unconsciously, they lead us to a better understanding of what William Faulkner called 'the unending conflicts of the human heart'.

In their heart of hearts, all human beings long for happiness. Establishing relationships with others, the principal source of achieving this objective, is an intrinsic part of this effort. The unconscious fears and hopes buried deep in our inner mind govern most of our actions and choices in life. Any creative approach to deal with and refine them can perhaps only be made in the language of the arts, and fictional works are the primary route to that subterranean self.

Works of fiction provide a unique way of probing the baffling emotional conflicts of the human heart. I believe that our choices and actions in life take shape, more than anything, by the experiences of life we undergo. And, reading a work of fiction that touches our heart is experiencing life, albeit by proxy. It takes us deep into the subconscious recesses of the mind and refines our emotional responses and relationships.

One of the most important parts of human life is the relationship between a man and a woman. And, unlike most other species, sexual aspects of various subtleties play a significant role in this relationship. Fearful of the intricacy and power of sexual passion social customs forbid any overt expression of this natural impulse. My effort in some of these stories has been to present the creative nourishment that flows from a relationship between a man and woman who love each other.

The freer and seemingly undisciplined paths of fictional tales offer glimpses of magic between two people, which is life's choicest gift. The emotive ties between a man and woman depicted in such creative writing enrich our vision of this relationship. The glory of a male-female bond, which is functional, emotional, and erotic, as was found by Dostoevsky with his second wife, is the greatest fulfilment that life can bring to anyone.

Fictional works suggest reassessment of the values we live by. Traditions offer stability in opposition to the risks of freedom and liberation. The ecstasy and ethereal fragrance of love is often not taken too kindly by traditional customs. But a resurgence of spirit inspired by love invariably tries to find answers to the real issue at stake: where does the ultimate responsibility of the individual lie? In preserving life, no matter how insipidly lived, or in accepting personal answerability for one's own emotional, physical, and intellectual well-being?

Sharat Kumar

The White Marble Burzi

The chowkidar did not have any, nor could he get it from the village which was far away from the fort. So finally there was no bedding at all and we used her saris and the curtains which we removed from the windows. It was cold when the wind blew through the broken window panes of the old palace as the mornings approached when she always abandoned herself to me just before dawn, and it was not because of the cold. She was unpredictable. We were embarrassed when the chowkidar brought the morning tea for he might have heard the ancient bed creak. I could not make her out, not in those five days, nor even now when I dream about her. I remember that unseen form only from touch for even in the mornings she would not let the covers fall. And now when I visit the palace, I often see her, as young as she was then, wandering over the ramparts of the abandoned fort in the moonlight. I create with my mind what the eyes never saw but the touch had known, and the heart led the imagination on.

The Betwa flows some distance away from the fort. Rivers change course over the years, and we do not know if the river was any closer to the fort when Bir Singh had built it some three centuries ago with the money and glory he received for killing Abul Fazal at the behest of Emperor Jehangir. The forest stretches far to the south. It is held by the bend in the river where ruins of the *chatris* in the royal cremation ground rise above the trees. The river flows swiftly over rocks and boulders. On moonlit nights one can see its frothy turbulence beyond the dark stretch of the forest from the marble burzi of the palace.

The village guides narrate the gory story of the murder of Abul Fazal to the rare visitor, as if to atone for the glory which could not obliterate its origins even with the building of two splendid temples whose spires rise to great heights to the west of the palace. The blue-tiled walls of the Jehangiri palace in the east shine in all their splendour as the sun rises above the white marble burzi of Bir Singh's palace. The burzi overlooks the landscape from a high point above the solid walls of the fort, almost overhanging the deep moat which has no water any longer. At nightfall, after the lonely chowkidar puts out his lantern at the far end of the fort, an eerie silence broken only by the occasional howling of jackals engulfs the landscape with its desolate buildings looming high above the flat plains.

"No one stays here," the chowkidar said as we declared our intention to spend a week at the fort. "It is better to stay the night at the forest bungalow four miles away." The *tonga* which had brought us from the station had already left, signifying our determination to stay. A generous tip did it finally. The Bundela chowkidar with his proud handlebar moustache, the lone custodian of the fort on a pittance from the archaeological department, even agreed to cook meals for us. I think he was fascinated by Aparna. Vibrating through all her elegance and finery was a wild exuberant spirit which reached out to men instantly. I wondered till the last day if she was ever conscious of it.

We walked to the monuments, photographing and taking notes all day long. It was meant to be research for a joint project, the history of the fort and the artistic linkage of its architecture to the traditions of the medieval period. I do not remember who had suggested the theme. The idea was attractive and it had not taken us long to plan the trip. I know now that both of us had reasons of our own, deeper than the love of research. The time and the project had merely fitted into the inevitable flow of events.

Aparna lived an exciting life. There were lively discussions at the gatherings in her house. She attracted intelligent people of diverse character, mostly much older than herself, and was constantly falling in and out of love. I often wondered how she felt about love.

"The word 'Eros' must have originated from 'Rasa', or vice versa. Why do people feel so squeamish in discussing Eros? Don't the *Tantriks* consider it the essence of life?"

"The great Shankaracharya had to experience *Kama* before he could defeat Mandana Mishra's wife in the shastrartha at Maheshwar."

"Researches in America suggest that women reach sexual prime only in their mid-thirties."

"The *nayikas* of the Indian tradition seem to reach their prime at eighteen. The Shilpa Shastra's formula—moon-breasted, swan-waisted, elephant-hipped may not quite work at thirty-five. The fruit apparently ripens early in a warmer climate."

"Centuries before William Blake, the Indian artists had achieved an unsurpassed mastery of the dark unconscious, the instinctive, and the emotional. They had learnt to represent it in their art as the core of human existence."

Discussions continued late into the night. We would come away enchanted, if not with the conversation then always with the lively presence of our young hostess. Twenty-eight years was not too young for a woman who lived as intensely as Aparna did. It just happened from the way life came to her, with little choice on her part. Psychologists would have us believe that most creative people have an unhappy childhood. Does that give them the intensity? The penetrating search? Even the strength to go on with the search? And what of the fears and the insecurity which remain with you for a long time. Does the intensity arise from the erotic impulse unable to find a fulfilling release, no matter how much physicality you may indulge in?

"I have been here before," she said dreamily. The outlines of the Jehangiri palace were silhouetted against the skyline as the moon rose above the ramparts of the fort. After the day's wanderings, we had climbed to the marble *burzi*. It had the best view, and always a breeze. The landscape stretched below us.

"Emperor Jahangir stayed here a full month." She went on, "He had a cruel mouth and his lips curved hard as he watched the girls dancing. Men are bad lovers even when they are emperors. They never give much of themselves to women."

The moonlight fell on her. The white marble of the *burzi* had a gentle luminous quality against the darkness of the forest. She had marvellous hands—tapering, clean, delicate, soft as her face, and it was an enchantment just to look at them. A peculiar grace illumined her features when she spoke. Her nose would move ever so slightly, and her cheeks curved above her open lips. Her eyes had a magical radiance. I was ensnared. It must have been the moonlight.

"There was dancing here, the courtyard was lit up with huge oil lamps. Festivities went on for a whole month." She stared into the darkness of the palace. "Beautiful women dressed in all their finery to charm men, and men proudly narrated the feats they had performed to win the women. But the yearnings of the woman's heart remain unfulfilled through the centuries. The journey continues, searching and searching. If all joy, the whole universe, is inside us, and if life can perpetuate itself only with the love of a man and a woman, isn't love the source of all things?"

I dared not touch her. She was in another world. My mind was filled with a resonating passion. I watched her bathed in the moonlight on the marble *burzi*, looking out into the forest beyond the walls of the fort. And later, when she was making the bed, I could see the outlines of her beautiful little bosom and the undulations of her hips. I stayed awake for a long time, all tense. But sometime at night she came back from wherever she had been, and was marvellous just before the dawn. She was a different person, warm and uninhibited with a carefree lilting laughter. It was sheer good luck that the chowkidar was late with the morning tea. She kissed me when he came finally, and pushed me off the bed.

We went to bathe in the river that morning. She looked lovely. Over her Rajasthani skirt she wore a red silk blouse which fell in such soft lines on her body, in such relief and such contours. She laughed as she slipped over the pebbles. The water was pleasantly cool and fresh. We found a pool behind a huge rock.

"I don't want to wet my dress," she said, "Will you

keep watch while I take off my clothes and bathe? And don't look."

"It will be difficult," I said, "but I will try."

"How hard will you try?"

"Not very hard."

She pushed me into the water and jumped in without removing her clothes. I splashed water on her till her eyes were red and she cried. We picked pebbles. She found some really beautiful stones. We sat on the boulders watching the fish swim in clear pools of sparkling water. And then we walked in the forest for a long time drying our clothes in the morning breeze.

I could not believe she was the same hypersensitive person looking forever for a perfect relationship. The elusive visions of her ideals made the relationships deeply searching and insecure, but also imbued them with a rare flavour and intensity. She noticed flaws in herself in relationship with others, and in others in their relationship with her. She questioned away her whole wishful scheme of things. It isn't the thing, but it must be, and it won't be. The torment had gone on.

There is, perhaps, an inbuilt limit to the emotional intensity a human being can cope with, independent of the dictates of the will. She was tired and wanted to stop and rest, and to make compromises. She had not yet learnt that compromises were inevitable, and perhaps the only way to defeat the compromises from defeating you was to be mischievous and playful with them, as with all important things, if you were ever to win.

It could be that she felt that I was overwhelmed by her and she would find it easy to handle me. I was more her age than most other people she was close to. In practical terms, I seemed to be the best choice she had to settle down with. But that practicality, good as it seemed, ate into the fragrance of her dreams of love. If the deliberate calculation, and the ever returning thoughts to it in weaker moments, could not be cleaned out of her system, what would the quality of the relationship really be?

Instinctively, without even understanding it, she knew that her strength lay in the purity of her mind, as it faced itself when there were no witnesses; when she did not answer for all the petty vulgarities that the mechanics of day-to-day life imposed on her, even didn't have to, as long as in the main she could look at and respect her own inner purity. The prize of all was the quality, of her private-secret-honest view of herself.

"The great philosophical and ethical truths that we mouth every day are also often mischievous tricks played by our subconscious mind, to prevent us from honestly looking into ourselves to see the way we really act and live." She remembered a conversation on her terrace. It had helped her understand the uneasy feeling she had with many men of the sharpest intellect.

"The unconscious is the dominating self. The body can make a monkey of the mind. In the frenzy of passion where does the intellect go? The body wants to surrender itself to another, to give. The mind, the speech, does not know how to."

"It is the ego which pulls you back. What if the surrender is not reciprocated? We hear and read endlessly that it is in giving that you receive. Yet when it comes to our own lives, ego overpowers and corrupts the heart with fear, and prevents unconditional giving."

"If you are too hard on the body, it fights back to clog the mind. Without coming to terms with the body, you cannot prevent the unpredictable breakdown of your rational system."

They had gone on to discuss the sublimation of bodily passion. There was a clinical quality to the discussion. Aparna sat fascinated. I looked at her and wondered how it would feel to hold her in my arms. The proximity of her body clouded my mind and I could not concentrate to keep up with the discussion.

"Doddering old fools," I thought, resentful at being left out of the conversation. "Their minds more dead than their bodies. Drumming up the intellectual jargon to make up for their weakening bodies and the pressures of desire."

Aparna was absorbed in the discussion. A life of the mind attracted her. And yet there were attractions of the senses. Would the world of the mind fulfil her? Her body yearned to be touched, to be played with, it longed for a commitment to the world of the senses, to a home, to children, to a permanency of love. Could she sublimate desire? Wouldn't that leave her all dried up, no matter what other rewards she gained. The barrenness would show on her face. Her manner would acquire a harsher quality, Even her voice would lose its melodious tone. Didn't the music of life come from love making, caring, giving, receiving? If the juices of her heart and body dried up what other compensation could she really have? One could drug oneself with external activity somnolently. But that did not stop the corruption, the coarsening of one's inner system which sapped the strength. Ultimately, didn't all joy even courage, spring from the aesthetic-erotic elements of life?

The sun had climbed high when we reached the palace. It was a cool and clear day heralding the onset of winter. Aparna wanted to photograph the big temple which had some splendid panels of rare carvings. She asked the Bundela chowkidar to serve an early lunch.

"Chilli soup, chilli meat, and chilli saag," she repeated the unalterable menu laughingly to him. Cooking was not the chowkidar's forte. He cooked, adding large quantities of chillies to every dish, hoping to improve the taste for the memsahib who had bowled him over. She really liked his handlebar moustache.

"It is so picturesque," she told me, "It adds such vigour to his wiry frame. Why don't you grow a moustache?"

It was her unmistakably mischievous playful style. She instinctively reacted to every opportunity for charming her men. Intellectual discussions were all very well, the real flavour of human relationships came from the quality of subconscious responses, from the instinctual gestures. I had never met anyone with a better instinct to react at the opportune moment.

For the first time ever, I heard her talk about God that afternoon. It was not a weary spirit looking for refuge. She had continued in her cheerful mood. But human moods, as I know now, so often superimpose themselves on the earlier moods—over so much thought that has gone on before—that it is not possible to gauge the causes leading to an event only from the mood of the moment.

We had climbed to a high point on the temple to take the photographs. The foothold was narrow and it made me giddy to look down from that height. The terrace below was paved with grey stones. The stones were smooth. They were not jagged or uneven. I could see the flower bed of marigolds on the terrace below. Aparna was looking down when I caught her hand.

"The pain would be sharp and sudden if one fell," she said. "The fall would break the neck. It would not be slow, and everything would soon be over. The stones will rise up to meet you."

A shiver ran though me, I held her firmly, and said, "Aparna, what nonsense is this?"

"It is god's house," she said. "One would go straight to heaven, to eternal happiness, like the old women who die on the *ghats* of Varanasi."

We came down and took some more photographs. There were some erotic panels half way down.

"I like this temple. The gods are so friendly here. They even make love. They seem only slightly superior to us." She was looking at the panels. "I was once at the Notre Dame in Paris. It also has high towers. It is also a house of God. But I was terrified. I was overawed by the power of God. I felt that the mighty God of that imposing edifice was seeing through me with his sharp eyes and would soon expose all my sins and punish me. The gods of this temple don't seem to worry so much about sin. They will let me keep my secrets."

"Crazy woman," I thought. "She is totally neurotic." I held her hand. It was warm and delicate. I looked at her slender form so close to me. I thought of the delicious mornings when she had given herself to me so beautifully.

"Aparna," I said my heart pounding wildly, "Why don't you get married?"

She looked at me silently and then smiled.

"Will you marry me?" she laughed. "Don't you think I am totally neurotic?"

I froze in my steps. She was capable of anything. I held both her hands and raised them to my lips instinctively. It was not a ritual.

"Yes! I will. Anywhere. Anytime." I was breathless.

She laughed again and took away her hands. "We could have a Gandharva vivah right hare. I am lucky the Betwa has so little water and the fish are small, they won't swallow my ring."

She stopped abruptly. Raising her camera she took a few steps backward to focus it on me. I felt her eyes looking at me searchingly though the lenses. It seemed an eternity before she took the photograph.

"You are sweet," she said. "If we stay together you will divorce me even before we get married."

"You can trust me," I heard myself saying, my words beginning to sound ridiculous.

She smiled at me. She clicked another photograph.

"I was reading a novel by Heinrich Boll last week," she said, "about an estranged wife in a hotel room, in bed with her husband attempting a reunion." Aparna was speaking calmly now. "She keeps looking out of the window all night at a neon sign on a pharmacy, blinking : You Can Trust Your Druggist."

"Will you be my druggist?" she said almost affectionately, "Will you drug me to happiness?"

"Aparna", Aparna," I pleaded desperately. "You must be sensible. What are you doing to yourself?"

She was strong-willed and sensitive The tension of the combination, unrelieved by faith or humour, was hard on her. Insecure people long for a great deal of intimacy—physical, emotional, even spiritual. Oblivious to this, imprisoned, as if by her acute sensitivity into a rarified world, she was trapped at a subtler level. She did not care to possess any one. She found that heavy on the soul and ultimately destructive. All earth-bound things, responsibility and morality, were heavy though they preserved and stabilized life.

Detachment was light, even immorality was. Light things pulled you way above yourself if you could take the elevation. You could generate much more at a higher level if you could. You risked all too much and could end up all wasted. But life had come to her that way. There was no choice.

We walked back slowly through the village bazaar. Aparna photographed some children who ran behind her, laughing and giggling, fascinated by her and her camera. A village belle peeped out of her window and caught her fancy. Aparna went into the courtyard and soon had all the women around her.

"Look," she said to me, "she was married at fifteen. She already has a baby."

The women were admiring her necklace. "They want to know why I don't wear *sindur*," she said again.

The light was fading. The evening was coming on. Dark clouds were gathering on the far horizon.

"Let's go back," I said.

She had an intelligent mind. She could reason and rationalize. She also had a mysteriously penetrating sense for the subtleties of feelings. Many children also have it, a God-given gift lasting only for a few years of early life. They discriminate and respond so well to different shades of feelings, knowing instinctively where their safety lies. Safety lay in emotional relationships. She also knew it. And then there were other centres that took shape in your body and in your emotions as the years passed. The intellect enhanced you, it also diminished you. The world of emotions rested on faith. In that inner world, in the deeper, darker recesses of the heart, reason and intellect—untempered by faith—destroyed more than they could create.

We walked in silence. I watched her walking with an unsteady pace. The fort loomed ahead of us.

"You did not give me an answer," I said.

She stopped. She looked up at the gathering clouds and said "I want a baby." And then she went on slowly, "If I had a baby twelve years ago, he would already be my friend. We could do things together."

Suddenly I was angry. "By now you would have made the boy a neurotic wreck. Don't you ever think of anyone else but yourself?"

And then I was sorry for my words. There was no way to retrieve them. We walked on in silence.

She had wanted to come to terms with her conflicting pulls. She wanted to love, to respect, to fondle and to hold sacred a relationship: but she also had to contend with the conflicting pulls of her mind. She could not force herself. The calculation did not work. And yet, without some calculation it was not possible even to preserve the purity of all that she held precious, to keep it from corruption which advanced all the time as the years passed.

It rained that night and it was cold. The rain blew through the broken window-panes. We could smell it in the room. Aparna had caught a chill. I did not touch her. She lay in bed, looking miserable and unwell with a tense expression on her face. She had not slept a wink.

The weather cleared in the morning. It was still cold. I gave her tea in bed and took her hand to count the pulse. I sat near the bed. She smiled at me weakly. She was not all there. The chowkidar brought hot milk for her breakfast. I had told him that she was not well.

"You have a slight fever," I said, "I must get some blankets from the village, the cleanest possible."

I gave her an aspirin and said again, "We can leave tomorrow if you are well."

She did not respond.

The village was far from the fort. I moved from house to house. The village folk were still using their thick cotton sheets. Their low-roofed mud houses were much warmer than the high rooms of the palace.

I had finished the first round of the houses. There were no blankets and I was trying to find a clean quilt when the chowkidar came, his face all ashen. He spoke only a few halting words. My mind leaped to the white marble *burzi*. There could be no doubt. The height was too great for any doubt.

The villagers were already in the moat when we got back. I stood by the road. There was no point in going down now. The police would come soon. Nothing could be touched. There was nothing to touch any more. A postmortem report would have to be made.

The white marble *burzi* overhanging the moat was lit by the morning sun. I looked up. A piece of cloth, a sari we had used as our bedding, was fluttering in the breeze. I went up with the chowkidar. You could not see her from the marble *burzi*. Some bushes overhanging from the sides of the moat blocked the view. The dry bed of the moat looked surprisingly like the terrace we had seen the previous day looking down from the temple. There were even some wild flowers. The white marble *burzi* was at a much greater height though.

In the bedroom there was a sheet of her thick note-paper prominently left on the table. She had pressed down a corner of the paper carefully with a book to prevent it from flying away in the breeze. It was a brief note signed neatly in her meticulous handwriting, dated, and the time had also been recorded. She did not want the police to bother me. She had been as efficient as ever. In her own way she had been fond of me.

I came away after two days. The chowkidar brought the *tonga* for me on his own. He was not even cooking the food any more. There seemed to be no need for it. There was nothing more to be done.

Over the years, I have often gone back to Bir Singh's old palace and watched the frothy turbulence of the Betwa beyond the forest. I walk through the forest to the river bed. The water is clear and I see the fish in small pools of sparkling water.

It is an old story now. And it is not good to live in the dreams of a dead person, in the visions of a mirage which can never come back to life. But perhaps this is not true. People remain as you want them to be. They are dead when they are alive. And still living when you cannot touch them any more. I see her in the sparkling waters of the Betwa and on the ramparts of the fort, and the vibrations rise through the landscape to permeate the spirit with their precious beauty which lives forever.

***

My Life

Mother is seriously ill and I have been coming to the hospital for the past seven days. Her hair had turned white when she was only fifty. But her long white tresses still have a fine lustre. The nurse sponges her every morning and combs her hair neatly. Mother's condition has been worsening for the past few days. Earlier this evening when her blood pressure was falling, the doctor had to prick several times to find a vein to give her an intravenous injection. The doctor said that medicines are not fully effective when a person is so old. I am sixty-five years old myself.

"She will have an uncomfortable night", I thought as I slumped into the easy chair.

"These may be required tonight", the nurse said as she examined the oxygen cylinders.

I stare blankly at the cylinders. Sixty-five years is a long time. Above the oxygen cylinders, the electric wires from the light switch extend up to the ceiling. It is an old fashioned building and the ceiling is supported by thick wooden beams—like the ceiling of my house in the university. Thirty years at the university seem to belong to a remote past. For some time now, my memories have been getting blurred. I do not even make any attempt to focus them. Somehow I have lost the capacity to concentrate my energies in a specific direction. In my house at the university, mother had a room which opened onto the lawn. During the winter vacations when I held extra classes on the lawn, mother always sent sweets for my students. With time, the fullness of those years now lies buried in my memory. In the last seven days at the hospital, I have begun to feel that sixty-five years is a very long time.

"The sheets are wet", the night nurse said, "Please call the ward-boy."

There is total stillness in the ward corridor. The ward was not so silent in the previous seven nights because mother was often restless. Today she seems exhausted. I wish something would disturb this silence and break the chain of images passing through my mind.

For some time now, I have been trying to control my mind—to prevent it from wandering. I make deliberate efforts to forget many things. This year I even forgot the anniversary of my wife's death. I used to observe a fast on that day, and perform a *havan* in the evening with my son and daughter sitting beside me. This routine had continued unchanged for the past 18 years. Even after losing faith in God and religious rituals, I could not give up performing a *havan* on that one day of the year. I have lost the capacity to make any firm resolutions. Ever since I was a child, I have liked the fragrance of Samagri. Perhaps I continued performing the *havans* for this reason. I used to think about my wife on that day. Those days stand out in my memory. She was fond of flowers and our garden always had the most beautiful roses. Long after she was gone everything in our house was full of her presence. She died so young, in the fullness of life—long before commencement of years of doubt and drift. For a long time I had preserved her letters as a treasure. Now they lie locked up with my other papers in the big steel trunk.

"Sheets", the ward-boy was fast asleep on his chair at the end of the corridor. I shook him, "The nurse wants some fresh sheets."

It is five years since I retired from the university. And I want to write a few books about all that I learnt in my life. These books will be my last link with life. They will give meaning to my last years. Only, I want to forget everything else. My wife has gone. My son and my daughter are not dependent on me, nor I on them. Mother is going now. Memories of the past have receded far into the background and I do not want to be overwhelmed with the weight of memories. I want to do my work. This alone can give me satisfaction. By getting absorbed in this work, I can forget myself.

"Please telephone the doctor", the night nurse had come out of the room, "The patient's blood pressure is falling again."

Beyond the window near the telephone table, the night is pitch dark. Silence pervades the corridor. Perhaps no other serious case has been admitted to the private ward. My son Vinay had called to say that he would visit the hospital in the evening. Hearing the sound of a car horn, I looked out of the window. But it is somebody else's car.

I have an easy relationship with my children. Often I tell my friends with pride that life has changed a lot in the past decades, and one can keep one's balance only through understanding the new situations of a new age. My relations with my son and daughter are cordial. When I look back to my youth, I often wonder how impersonal life has become today. Before I retired from the university, life had flown steadily with an easy continuity, and any new development took an age to make an impression on my consciousness. But after retirement, I seem to have developed a sharpened awareness. Sometimes, in spite of the hustle and bustle of this big city, I feel myself enveloped by a sense of vacuum. But I have to write my books and finish my work.

I no longer have my house at the university. My new house is a long distance away but I often walk to the library. I have got accustomed to walking under the long rows of trees in the university, and if I do not go there several times a week, I feel that I am missing a part of my life. With many closing chapters of life, I feel that mother's room will soon be empty too. My old servant Bir Singh and his wife look after me very well. Bir Singh remembers many incidents from Vinay and Sunila's childhood. Often he stands near the dinner table and tells me old stories.

"Papa! You constantly find fault with me. Nobody says anything to Vinay", Sunila always complained.

"There is a difference between boys and girls, my child. You cannot copy Vinay in everything," I would tell her. But I always felt that I did not bring her up properly. Often I think that I should have remarried. Sunila was very young then. After my wife's death, our house lost the harmonious grace of a home. "There was a deficiency which I could not fill. Perhaps it was not even possible for me to do so.

"Your children have too much freedom," my friends and relatives often reprimanded me. "You are not enforcing the discipline a father should. At least keep the girl in control."

But I could not discipline the girl at all. Sunila is now more of a friend than a daughter to me. She is my darling. She knows my habits, weaknesses, and preferences better than I do myself. She is twenty-seven years old now and I wish she would decide to get married. She lives by herself in another town. Her maternal grandfather left her a legacy which she inherited on becoming an adult.

"Papa! No one likes me" She always laughs the subject away, She still has an impish gleam in her eyes. But sometimes I feel that her innocent laughter is now giving way to seriousness. Perhaps I should have arranged a marriage for her when she was twenty. Sunila was pretty and wealthy, and there were many proposals. My relatives were annoyed with me, but it has never been possible for me to compel Sunila to do anything she did not like. Keeping up with my relatives has always been a difficult task for me. After the death of my wife, the university and the students had filled my life. And by the time I retired the gap between my relatives and I had widened so much that I had neither the capacity nor the possibility, or even the inclination, to bridge it. Now I only want to be left in peace to do my work. But it is strange that I have been able to do much work in the last two or three years. As I sit at my desk my mind seems to wander off in many directions in spite of my efforts to concentrate.

"Bir Singh, you should not let Papa drink so many cups of tea," Sunila complains when she comes to visit me every two or three months.

"Munni! You should get married and take Saheb to your house", Bir Singh replies.

Sunila asks me as she pours out the tea, "Papa, why don't you go and spend a few days with Bhaiya?"

I look at the black *bindi* on her forehead, "Sunni, talk about yourself. Why involve your Bhaiya in it?"

There is an age difference of eight years between Vinay and Sunila. But the difference in years seems to have widened with the passage of time. Often I feel that while Vinay has moved to settle on the solid crust of the earth, Sunila has continued her journey away from the surface, in an ethereal world. Perhaps I am wrong. I have developed a sharper consciousness of my own mistakes and complaints against myself. But I have no grudges against Vinay. He is a dutiful son, if not so much of a friend to me. For a long time he worked in a distant town but recently he has moved to the same city. We have been trying to rebuild our relationship on a new basis. I carried out my duty towards my children as best as I could, and now we can only be friends. I would like to go for a long walk with Vinay under the rows of tall trees at the university. I would like to sit with him as I do with Sunila, sipping tea and talking as the evening closes around us. But Vinay leads an organized and busy life, and this has not been possible.

"Bir Singh, why don't you sweep the cobwebs from the rooms? The house looks so shabby." Vinay makes it a point to visit me once a week after office. He lives in a posh new colony at the other end of town. Mother always complained that Sunila never spends any time with her even when she stays overnight at the house. Vinay never forgets to spend some time with mother.

"Papa, what is Sunila doing these days?" But I cannot respond. "She did not even meet me the last time when she was in town. Papa, you must tell her that she is no longer a child. There should be some order and stability in her life."

I can never make Sunila understand anything. In our conversation most of the talking is done by her. I have never been able to reprimand her. I am told that I have spoilt her. Sometimes I wonder myself if she would have grown up differently if she was disciplined more strictly and if she had not inherited her grandfather's legacy. I try to imagine what she might have been. But when I see how other girls of her age live, I am no longer very sure how spoilt my Sunila is.

A peculiar change seems to have come over in my analysis of life since I retired from the university. Earlier, I saw everything with clarity and was able to make a distinction between right and wrong, between truth and untruth. But now I begin to examine both sides of an issue, and find it difficult to arrive at a definite conclusion. Perhaps it is because of this that I no longer have any faith in the existence of God or any other supernatural force though I had believed in them earlier. I, however, observe, that many retired people of my age who had found no time for God or religion right through their working lives have suddenly developed an efflorescent faith.

There was a time when men and women went to Varanasi in their old age hoping to go straight to heaven at the end of their lives. The other world has never interested me. I am still in this world, and I would like to lead a good life by understanding the situations of this world correctly. Instead of dreaming about the other world, I would like to do my work in this world. I would like to leave behind the knowledge which I have gathered in the last thirty or forty years of my life by documenting it in an orderly manner. My work alone can offer me solace in the last years of my life.

"Papa! Your books and philosophies have relevance only in the classroom. They bear no relationship to the real world." Sunila would have long discussions with me every time she read a new book.

"Sunil, all things do not have an overt relationship. The basic purpose of education is to develop the mind so that an individual can think for himself in a disciplined manner."

"Which of your students is capable of thinking for himself?" She would ask.

I was inclined to agree that many of my students could not think for themselves. I had observed that in the last fifteen years the intellectual calibre of my students had declined. Perhaps good students no longer enrol for philosophy and literature. Science and technology have a greater attraction. I think that for breaking new ground in any field it is necessary that man's mind should reach out beyond the limited circle of established conventions. A bold freedom of spirit and thought is essential for any creative contribution. In this age of glittering material progress, a balanced emphasis should be placed on the teaching of philosophy, languages, and the arts. Such an education is necessary not only for restoring a sense of harmony between the inner and external life of man, but perhaps also for the progress of science and technology.

"There is endless hair-splitting in your philosophical discussions on the nature of matter, life and existence. I do not understand what purpose this serves. Centuries ago if the same intellectual efforts had been applied to the development of natural sciences, such abject poverty would not have existed in our country today."

But such conversations with Sunila are many years old now. Perhaps she has also forgotten most of them. But I cannot erase them from my memory. She had a brilliant mind and often her remarks would leave me thinking. I am aware of the limitations of my subject. But I have spent my life in it and now I cannot turn to a new direction. I realize that no single discipline can be complete in itself. I feel that Sunila is frittering away her abilities in the confusions arising from the lack of a single direction. Sometimes I think that if her economic circumstances had not been so easy, the compulsions of material existence would have disciplined her, and perhaps prevented a directionless dissipation of her energies. Now she is my friend, and for the past few weeks, I have been so full of doubts myself that I cannot offer advice to anyone.

"Wake up, Papa! The doctor is calling you," I had dozed off in the quiet darkness of the corridor. It was past midnight already.

"I was at an official dinner which finished very late," Vinay was waking me up, "I called Sunila long distance. She is coming by the night train,"

I told the doctor that mother had already been given two injections earlier in the evening to raise her blood pressure. Mother lay absolutely still.

"We cannot give her more injections," the doctor said. "We will put her on oxygen. Let us watch her condition overnight."

I feel that mother would have a difficult night. I have had such feelings for the last few nights and they have been compelling me to think about my life. I have nothing to complain about life and I am not afraid of death. Perhaps I have got accustomed to go on living and I do not relish the prospect of a change. And I want to finish my work. My only complaint is against myself, that I am not able to work as well, and with as much speed, as I would have liked to.

"Your son is very competent", my friends compliment me, "He will be very successful". I am unable to measure success or failure. I have lived sixty-five years and in this long period I have observed the lives of many people. And now I am no longer able to understand who is a success and who a failure.

My son has changed a lot. I tried to give my children the best education I could. What more could I have done? Many years ago I was surprised and pained to learn that Vinay felt that I had not done the best for him. But it is an old story now and he must have forgotten it.

"You are making a mistake," my friends used to tell me. "The social system does not change easily. Everything will continue as before." And in fact everything has continued as it was before." But in those days I thought that many changes would take place. I still think that many changes should take place. But my friends, and now many of my young friends, do not think so.

"The world has always gone on like this," they say philosophically. "And it will always continue in the same manner."

"At one time man had a tail. Where are your tails now?" I feel like shouting at them. But I am sixty-five years old now and cannot shout much. In fact I have never been able to shout. I have taught philosophy and all I want now is sit at the desk in my room and write a few books.

"Papa, social changes are a part of the historical process. They can only be seen in the overall perspective of the progress of human civilization," Vinay used to say a long time ago. I know it is absurd not to shout yourself and expect others to speak for you. But there are many things which I understood too late. If I had learnt them earlier, perhaps I could have done something.

"Man has only one life to live." Vinay must now have forgotten his remarks of fifteen years ago. I am quite aware that God has not granted two lives to any man so far. I also know that Vinay has now travelled far from those who make a noise. But I observe a strange phenomenon these days; man twists his life into several isolated compartments, and lives many parallel lives at the same time.

"Papa, it is time for Sunila's train. I will go and fetch her." I can hear the sound of the car as Vinay drives away.

I go into mother's room. She is still under oxygen. The nurse keeps noting her blood pressure at short intervals. The night light is on and I slide into the arm-chair.

"I will ask them to keep a bright light burning in my room," I thought. I cannot stop my work. In any case, I sleep better under a bright light. Sunila could never sleep in my room even as a child because of this habit of mine. For sometime now, I have noticed that Sunila often takes Bir Singh's daughter in her lap and plays with her. My mind floods with doubts and I start thinking about Sunila. I wish I could bestow on her some part of the fullness of my long years. I feel that my children have travelled far away from me. In their growing years, I had provided them protection and security. I gave them opportunities for a healthy growth by keeping them away from the pressure of life when they were young; the kind of opportunities which I would like every young child to have under a new social order. I do not know why my children have drifted away. I am tired. I could not sleep properly last night. And mother is lying so still in her bed.

I feel that I am floating in the air—beyond the ventilator—out under the open sky. The first rays of sunshine are beginning to light up the eastern sky. The earth is full of criss-crossing lines and shapes. It seems to be moving away. Clouds drift across the sky. Now they engulf me. I think it will rain and the rain will carry me back to the earth. There is a mist all around and I am enveloped in its milky brilliance.

It was dawn when Sunila woke me. Mother's hands are absolutely cold. Perhaps their ever comforting warmth that I had known from my earliest days will not be back again.

Saturday, Sunday

When he was tying the carrier bag to the rear mudguard of his motor cycle, he was surprised that it had so much space. The bag took in two white bed sheets, a ground sheet, a bag of groceries, a frying pan, one book, an empty shoulder bag, two blankets, and a small tent with a telescopic pole. It was two o'clock when he reached the petrol station. He was glad that he could finish his preparations and leave on time in spite of getting held up at the grocery shop for half an hour.

The road was wide. But there was a continuous stream of slow moving trucks and cars, and he could not drive his motor cycle as fast as he would have liked to. At one point he followed a city bus for more than a mile. The crowded road did not permit any overtaking, and the black exhaust of the bus filled his lungs. Thin clouds floated in the sky. A wet sea breeze blew and when the sun was covered by clouds, it was not so hot. Small houses lined the road. Outside the houses, children played in dust near the road even though the doors of the house were only twenty feet from where the buses plied.

The city thinned out further on, and there were attractive modern factories along the road now which were surrounded by trees and manicured lawns. These were the new factories which did not produce any fumes to pollute the air. Beyond the city limit, the smoke-belching buses of the local transport service were not on the road any more. The clouds formed big patterns in the sky. The sea breeze now blew against his back and he could breathe more easily on his fast-running motor cycle. He felt the freshness of the air and filled his lungs with deep breaths.

After driving for an hour and a half he stopped for a drink of water and discovered that he had forgotten to bring his water bottle. There was much less traffic on the road now. It was a highway connecting two cities and sometimes trucks coming from opposite directions raised a big cloud of dust which forced him off the tarmac. Small hills were now visible on the left hand side. After a while he turned into a narrow road going towards the hills, which ran through patches of green fields. Beyond the fields, the road climbed sharply into the hills covered with grass. It was the end of October and the monsoon had been over for a month. The grass was almost two feet high. The greenery of the rainy season wilted under the fierce sun. On the sunny slopes, the grass had turned pale yellow flecked with gold. Verdure had lingered in the shade. There were many patches of shrubs in the yellow expanse of grass which had retained their freshness despite a month of the bright sun.

The road wound into the hills and as it climbed the breeze turned cooler. The motor cycle raced up in the second gear and when he stopped for a rest to cool the engine, there was a chill in the air and he did not want to stand in the shade. It was almost four o'clock. It would be dark in two hours. He knew that another half hour would be required to reach the place where he was to leave his motor cycle.

Dark clouds had gathered in the sky but rain seemed unlikely. Below him, he could see that the road had come through a deep gorge. Across the gorge, far in the distance, there were small hills silhouetted by the sun behind them. The hills appeared blue through the mist. On the other side, the hill rose steeply and there was a pale evening light on its slopes. The grass had turned pink in places and it was obvious that the sun would soon scorch it a dry brown. The pink patches made delicate patterns on the sunlit slopes. He sat on the parapet near his motor cycle for a long time looking at the grass which had so many hues. It felt comforting to be sitting in the warmth of the sun. But it was nearly five o'clock and the sun was already low on the horizon.

The engine had cooled and the motor cycle could now climb in the third gear. After a while the road flattened out and he was driving through a plateau which spread out far into the distance. There were many small hills in the plateau, and near the horizon faint outlines of high mountains were visible in the fading light of the evening. Since there was a nip in the air, he buttoned up his jacket. He could now see a big lake some distance away from the road. Tall hills on the two sides of the lake were covered with green bushes.

He slowed down to look at the lake. He knew that the lake stretched into the plateau through a small gap in the hills. He looked for a footpath to go over the hills. But the sun was on the other side, and he could not spot the footpath in the dark shadow on the hill side.

There was a cluster of small houses some distance away from the lake. He stopped at a petrol pump ahead of the houses and settled with the petrol pump owner to park his motor cycle near the pump office building. A boy at the pump showed him a red gravelled path that led to the lake. He said that half way down the path he would find a wooden board with a marking that read "Jheel". A dirt road from there would take him to the lake through a jungle.

He slung the carrier-bag on his back, emptying some of the contents into his shoulder bag. After a short walk when he reached the dirt road it was a little past five o'clock.

He knew that the sun would set in an hour. And he wondered if it would rain at night. It occurred to him that not once in the last three hours had he thought about his job and daily routine. Thinking of the rain again, he was glad that he had decided to bring a ground sheet at the last minute.

The earth was red, and in places the footpath was overgrown with grass. He walked briskly for an hour before he reached the lake. As he walked through the tall grass on the edge of the lake, he realized that the road on which he had driven his motor cycle was now on the other side of the hill. It was after a long time that he had walked with a load on his back. His forehead was sweaty and he was hungry. When he bent down to drink the clear cold water of a small stream that flowed into the lake, he felt a closeness to the grass and earth.

The lake water was a clear blue, and the gravel around the water was red. He walked through the grass on the edges of the lake till the sun set. The lake stretched far into the plateau behind the hills. There was grass all around and a few bushes and trees stood at several places. The peaks of high mountains on the horizon were now covered with dark clouds. When he reached the bank of the river that flowed from the distant mountains into the lake, the sun had already set. He selected a clear patch of land near a big rock to pitch the tent, some distance away from the river. There were two trees near the river bank and he neatly cut some branches with his jack-knife to make pegs for the tent.

It took him a long time to pitch the tent. The telescopic aluminium pole had got stuck and it was a struggle to pull it out. He spread the ground sheet and then doubled a blanket on it. The other blanket was then lined with a white sheet and turned over at half length. He folded his raincoat neatly for a pillow. After making his bed, he dug a drain around the tent with his jack-knife to ensure that the water would not come in if it rained at night. Daylight was almost gone. After finishing with the drain, he collected some dry twigs and lit a fire and put some water in a mug to boil.

The first stars twinkled in the sky when he spread a towel on the flat rock near the tent and cut slices from the loaf of bread and opened a tin of sardines. While eating his sandwiches, he watched the stars appearing one by one in the sky as darkness crept on. He counted the early stars, but after a while the stars came out so fast that it was not possible for him to keep track of them. He was amused to see the interesting patterns the stars made in the sky. The moon had not yet risen. Afterwards, he made coffee with the water boiling on the fire. When he returned to the flat rock with his cup of coffee, darkness had fully enveloped the jungle. The wind had died down and there were no ripples in the dark waters of the lake.

As he washed the coffee cup and cleaned the flat tin of sardines, he heard the jackals howling all around. He stamped out the fire with a stone and sprinkled some water on the embers. He had heard that tigers often prowled in the area, but he knew that tigers and other wild animals rarely interfered with men unless they were provoked.

The night air was getting cold. He took off his jacket and trousers and folded them under the makeshift pillow of his raincoat. He left the flap of the tent half open and fixed a candle on the flat tin of sardines. Then he slid into his bed and drew the blanket lined with the white cotton sheet over him. In the candle light he opened a book which he had brought with him. But after a while he did not feel like reading and closed the book. He stretched himself in his bed and felt the pleasant warmth of the blanket. He was tired and soon he put out the candle.

He enjoyed the warmth of his clean sheets and the feeling of closeness to the grass and earth. Outside the half open flap of the tent, the sky was strewn with stars. He closed the flap and listened to the sounds of the jungle in the deepening night. Innumerable sounds of grass insects intermingled with the occasional baying of animals and the swish of the river emptying into the lake. He was tired and soon fell asleep.

When he woke up, the sun was already high above the hills. The lake reflected the sun like a mirror. He folded the blankets and the sheets neatly and secured the flaps of the tent, and decided to go for a long walk along the river bank. There was a faint breeze and he liked the feel of cool morning air on his body. The river was a small swift flowing stream and several times he waded through it looking for fish. After the walk when he returned to the tent, he lit the fire to boil two eggs and put some water to boil for coffee. He washed the mud from the jack-knife he had used the previous night to dig the drain around the tent, and cut four slices of bread. He ate his food leisurely and then washed the cup and knife, and put them in the bag. Then he stretched out in the sun on his ground sheet to read a book. The sun was strong and he took off his shirt to use it as a sun shade to avoid the glare on the white pages of the book.

Despite the cold breeze, his back was scorched in an hour. He closed the book and turned over to lie flat on his back with the shirt covering his face. When he woke up the sun was at zenith. He took off his clothes and walked to the lake. Tall, yellow blades of grass near the lake swayed in the breeze gracefully like a dancer. In the clear water of the lake he could see the stones and rocks under the surface. After the scorching sun, he loved the cold water soothing his body, and he swam far into the lake with steady long strokes. Later, he turned on his back and floated on the surface, paddling lazily with his feet. He shut his eyes for a long time to avoid the glare of the sun. When the clouds came up, he watched them drifting across the sky. The distant high mountains still appeared blue through the haze. Dark clouds hung low on the horizon. There was a possibility of rain towards the evening. He swam steadily for a long time in the cold water towards a black rock which jutted above the surface.

He was exhausted when he came out of the lake after his swim. He rubbed himself with his towel for a long time before putting on his clothes. Then he took out the remaining slices of bread and cut the pineapple tin neatly along the edges. After he finished eating, he washed the plates, knives and the tin. He left the clean empty pineapple tin in an open space near the lake for it to come in handy for any other visitor to the lake. He was sleepy after his long swim, and he spread the ground sheet and a blanket inside the tent and dropped off to sleep.

The sky was full of clouds when he woke up. He picked up his towel and went to the lake to wash his face. On coming back he pulled out the pegs of the tent, removed the telescopic aluminium pole, and folded the tent neatly into his carrier bag. It took him only a few minutes to pack his things. He kept his raincoat out and put it in his shoulder bag. The clouds hung so low in the sky that they appeared to be floating on top of the hills behind the lake. He watched the clouds and knew that such low clouds did not bring heavy rain. He could smell rain in the breeze blowing from the hills. The clouds were fluffy and the horizon had no sharp lines. It was as if the sky and the earth had come closer and merged into each other. There was an intimate quality to the atmosphere. It was very different from the vastness of the clear sky of the previous night.

It began to drizzle, and after he had put on his raincoat, he watched the rain falling in the lake. There were small waves in the water because of the breeze. The first drops of rain had brought out a fragrance from the parched earth. He walked slowly listening to the rain falling on the trees and watched the grass sway in the breeze. With his slow walk it took him two hours to reach the village where he had left his motor cycle. The rain had washed the tarred road a shining black. After tying the carrier bag to the rear mudguard, when he started the motor cycle, he saw that the road was wet. He drove slowly and it took him four hours to reach his room in the city.

Florence

Florence is severely burnt. She has been admitted to hospital and is in bad shape. As the news travelled to the office, a pall of gloom descended on everyone. She'd been married only the previous year. The incident was appalling, also intriguing. One does not hear of dowry squabbles among members of the Anglo-Indian community. And for that matter, Florence lived alone with her husband, not with his family. No mother-in-law, no brother-in-law, no sister-in-law. "She burnt herself in the bathroom with her own hands, man!" The loud voice of the telephone operator travelled to the office rooms.

The prospect of Florence resuming her duties appeared dim, and the personnel officer had asked the old telephone operator to take over the switchboard in Florence's place. The power was off—the perennial load-shedding—and the air-conditioning had also stopped. Through the open doors of the office rooms, one's gaze strayed to the switchboard. One remembered Florence, elegantly draped in a light lemon sari with a deep ochre-coloured border when she had come to sit at the switchboard for the first time. A flower was tucked under her thick bun of hair. Only that somewhat fair hair gave her away—yes, one could suspect her to be an Anglo-Indian. Not quite though. She could also have passed for a girl from one of those genteel Calcutta-Bengali families who were in a poor financial condition. The talk going round the switchboard drifted into the office. "The doctor says she has third degree burns. I must visit the hospital again. Florence is in a pitiable state. Her face is covered in bandages, her hair's all burnt, man!"

On days of load-shedding, Florence's voice often came through the same doors, in her elegant English, every word meticulously pronounced. Or in gracefully spoken chaste Bengali, Her lilting voice was so pleasant to the ear.

At 11, as per routine, the office peon Nurul brought three *biras* of *paan* from a shop beyond the main gate and placed them on the desk of Personnel Officer Das Babu. "Sir, Nimai Da requests three gate passes for the union members. They want to visit the hospital."

"*Choop! Sala log*," Das Babu suddenly flared up into a real temper. The first thing he had heard on entering the office that morning was the news of Florence's mishap. A paunch in the making, his hairline fast receding from a balding pate, the 45-year-old personnel officer was a self-proclaimed "anti-social element". Thrusting the *biras* of *paan* into his mouth and wiping the red juice from the corners of his lips with his finger, he yelled again. "*Sala log*! They called Indira Gandhi a whore when she was alive and then demanded three days leave to mourn her death. Let anyone live or die, it's a good pretext for them to run up to the party office."

"No sir they want to go to the hospital. The union has collected 3,000 rupees for Florence-*memsaheb*."

Last year after a continuous five-day-long haggle, which dragged on till 3 o'clock every night, Das Babu had succeeded in clinching the three-yearly agreement with the union. In recognition, the company had rewarded Das Babu with a car at the 'written down value'. While driving home in his newly acquired car one evening, Das Babu offered Florence a lift. Then, realizing her predicament in a rare flash of sensitivity, he had asked the peon Nurul to hop in along with another office boy. "What will the people say? Such a nice girl travelling alone with such a *badmash*!" Noticing the misery on Florence's face, Das Babu decided then and there that never again would he subject her to such a trauma. In fact, Das Babu was overwhelmed that day by a strange wish—to address the fatherless girl as *'bitiya'*. But he had kept his mouth shut lest his emotional upsurge caused him to spray *paan* juice over her dress.

Florence got a double increment for two successive years. "Sir, she is from Loreto Convent." Das Babu had strongly pleaded her case before the management every time.

"By God, you Bongs are bloody snobs!" the general manager had said good humouredly. "I hear it's a must for the chief minister of Bengal to be an Oxbridge. Nobody can pull down Jyoti Basu from his chair. There is no other Oxbridge in the Marxist party."

Before Florence's marriage, word had got round that Das Babu had made thorough enquiries through his friends, the OC of the police station of the locality, about Florence's fianceé, Robert, who was a sergeant with the Calcutta police. Das Babu wanted to know everything about his "character" and his "future prospects". Tired of his persistent probing, the OC had remarked that even the girl's *baba* would not have made such detailed investigations.

And now that same Robert hadn't visited the hospital as yet. He wasn't even home last night when the flames had engulfed her body. As the flames leapt up, it seems Florence had made an attempt to douse them with water. But the tap was dry. As usual, the municipality had turned off the water supply at night.

"The police are bastards," Das Babu fumed. "Their fathers are bastards and so are their sons! The department is such. You become a bastard the moment you join it. The English were an honest lot. Two hundred years ago they had inscribed the word 'bastard' in Latin on the badge fixed on policemen's helmets." Memories of past events tormented Das Babu, and his anger was no consolation. "What made such a lovely girl burn herself?

Why should anybody harm her?" Das Babu knew that Florence was the type who kept her woes to herself.

With her face wrapped in bandages and all her hair gone, it wasn't easy to recognize Florence. Her identity was now reduced to the numbered nondescript bed on which she lay. There was no resemblance between the figure on the bed and Florence as she had been. Still, there was life in her, her mind still worked. Images of the past floated in her mind.

Three-year-old Florence is playing on the lawn, her tiny feet shod in white shoes. She is wearing a blue frock, a colour so dear to her Papa. The mild sunshine of January's first Sunday is falling on the flowers blooming outside their Asansol house. Khokon and Ritu from the adjoining house have stealthily crept through the hedge to play with her. Khokon is running as he tries to fly a kite. Florence chases him with Ritu in tow.

"It's taken off! It's rising in the air!" Khokon is shouting. The kite is climbing in the sky.

"I-e-e-e"—Florence has slipped on a wet patch of lawn, Ritu is still running after Khokon, asking him to hand her the kite-string.

"Ayah!" Mummy's sharp voice rings out from her room which opens onto the lawn. Frightened, the children freeze in their steps. "How often have I told you not to let these native children in?"

"Dora! Really! How can you? Right in front of the children?"

Florence rises up in the air held by her Papa's arms. "I-e-e, "Florence is still sobbing as she sits perched on Papa's shoulder. "Good children don't cry. Look, you squashed an ant. Come catch that butterfly." Papa's strong arms toss Florence up in the air under the sparkling blue sky.

Florence likes the winter months of December and January. She loves Calcutta during these two months. In the festive weeks of Christmas and the New Year, there is no place to match Park Street. Sometimes the sky is covered by a dense dark smoke emitted by the old factories in Howrah across the Hooghly. But on most days a fresh cool breeze blows across the city and keeps the air clean. On such days, Florence loves to go to the *maidan*, visit the gardens, walk along the Strand on the bank of the Hooghly.

Robert has arrived in his blue police jeep to take Florence to the annual flower show of the Royal Horticulture Society. He knows she loves flowers. Florence rarely wears a skirt. She looks so elegant in a sari. People turn their heads to look at them. Robert's broad chest visibly expands with pride. There is no dearth of girls ready to fall for the tall handsome Robert, dressed in his police uniform. But Robert has eyes for no other girl. He says Florence is a great gift bestowed on him for some good deeds in a previous birth.

"Which flower do you like best?" Robert asks Florence.

On the day of their wedding, Robert comes to fetch Florence in a car decked with flowers of her choice. There is such a profusion of flowers that even the seats of the car aren't visible. Once, on her birthday, Papa had also filled her room with flowers and multi-coloured balloons.

Robert is tall and light-skinned like Papa. He has Papa's hair and the same blue eyes. But Florence can discern a note of sharpness in Robert's voice. She can't remember her Papa ever raising his voice. Sometimes Florence is scared of Robert. He is from the police. Bullying is his profession. But Papa was an engineer in the railway workshop, always quietly engrossed in his work. Like Mummy, Robert speaks in English most of the time. Papa spoke to Florence in Hindi, often in broken Bengali. And Mummy—she never wore a sari.

Returning from school, Florence runs up the stairs into the room to sit on Papa's lap. His protective arms enfold her. "Florence has now grown up. Too heavy to sit on Papa's lap."

"I *will* sit here." She puts her arms around Papa. "This is my place."

"I've told you so many times! Knock before you enter my room." Mummy's voice is sharp. "Don't disturb us. Go to your room."

Florence does not shut the door. She can hear Papa's voice from her room. "The loco workshop in Benaras is being expanded. A good chance of promotion."

"Benaras is a dirty, backward Hindu town. We can't live there."

"Going by you, the entire country is backward. One must think of one's future."

"We've no future in this wretched country. We can't live here. You're so adamant. We should have migrated long ago."

"Dora, we were born here, we were brought up here, we don't know any other country. If the Greeks, Scythians, Arabs and Mughals could live here for centuries, why can't we?"

"You are just being adamant for nothing. We could live so well in England or in Canada."

"Dora, nobody likes us in those countries. We won't fit in there. At least I won't."

"You are so light-skinned. Nobody will know the difference."

"But I will. Don't you understand? It's not a question of colour. We can be happy only in a culture that we were brought up in. In other countries we will be like fish out of water."

"Do you know what I've to put up with here? These wretched street urchins have become so bold. They yell 'Mem, Mem, three-legged mem' when I pass by."

"Dora, you deliberately live in an arrogant unreal world. Have you ever thought of your own attitude?

You behave like an English lady looking down on the natives."

Mummy gets terribly angry. Papa gets up and goes off to his room. Florence would not go to England or to Canada. She would live in India with Papa. Mummy wanted Florence to learn to play the piano. Florence would play the sitar.

"Mummy, what's an Anglo-Indian?"

"Foolish child! Always asking silly questions."

A few days later Florence asks the same question of Papa.

"Florence, let's go out for a walk," Papa says. Walking alongside Papa, holding his hand, Florence asks, "Papa, are Anglo-Indians not good people?"

"Florence, good and bad depends on how you look at things. If a man thinks good and talks good, he becomes good. And if a man thinks of bad things and talks evil, he becomes a bad man. A good man can be of any country, any colour, any caste, any religion. The same is true of a bad man."

"Papa, is Mummy an Anglo-Indian?"

Papa's rhythmic gait wavers for a moment and then a faint smile crosses his face. "Your mother's mama was English while her papa was an Indian. My father had come from England. He decided to live in India and married an Indian girl. This has been happening for centuries.

About 2000 years ago, Greeks had come to India and many of them decided to stay back in the country. And they were followed by many other communities, the Arabs and the Mughals among them."

"Papa, can you fly a kite?"

"Florence, when I was small, we lived in Lucknow. We used to fly many kites then. Lucknow is the city for kites. But now I have grown up, Grown-ups don't play with kites".

"Papa, what do the grown-ups play with?"

The doctor arrived to give an injection. Which is this nursing home? So neat and clean. Florence was shifted here last evening. Das Babu had come to visit her and walked beside her stretcher. "The company will bear all her medical expenses." He was speaking to Mummy. If one got the attention that one did on falling ill, no one would ever fall ill.

Robert has come—after a lapse of two days. Florence can see him. She can hear him. She can even understand why he did not come for the last two days, and how he must be suffering in his mind. Robert is so simple and open-hearted. It isn't difficult to understand him. "There's nothing to forgive, Robert," Florence wants to tell him. "You are so good. But our worlds were so different." She wants to talk to him but she cannot even swallow anything. The glucose drip is keeping her alive. Her whole body, even the face, is swathed in bandages.

She can hear. She can understand. She can even sense what Robert failed to say but which is written all over his face.

Florence is 12, Papa has been posted to the Chittaranjan Locomotive Workshop. Mummy likes the place because of its proximity to Calcutta. In the rainy season Florence loves to wander about in the open fields, inhaling the clean invigorating air. She looks with unending wonder at the dark rain clouds lit up by flashes of lightning. As the rain starts falling, she runs out of the house and comes back drenched. In spite of Mummy's repeated warnings that she would catch pneumonia, she has never fallen ill despite getting soaked in the rain so many times. But something strange has happened to her in the last two days. She feels so frightened at the sight of blood. She is bewildered. So much blood! And it would not even stop. People die when they lose so much blood. Mummy knows something but she just keeps looking at her without uttering a word. She tells Florence to lie down in her bed and covers her up with a sheet. Annoyed at her persistent queries, Mummy says, "You are growing up." Then she adds, "If you were a Hindu girl, they would have called you polluted and put your bed out in a corner."

Florence can hear Papa and Mummy arguing in Mummy's room. She can hear Papa's voice. "Straight and natural… explain normally… why not… her mind should be easy." A radio is on in the room, drowning most of the conversation. Florence is puzzled. What is her ailment? How did she pick it up? She is unable to understand anything. Her mind is troubled and she has not been able to sleep well for the past two days.

"Florence!" Papa's hand caresses her forehead. "How are you, my child?" He is sitting in a chair by her bedside, his face so gentle in the soft light of the table lamp. After a short silence, he says, "You are not sick, Florence. It is a natural process." Florence keep looking at his face. When Papa speaks, his eyebrows rise and his lips curl slightly upwards at the corner of the mouth. "When girls grow up their bodies undergo certain changes. This happens with all girls. It's a natural process of growth—as natural as my hair turning grey. Do you understand? Now put your books in order and go to school tomorrow. You are not ill in any way."

Florence did not understand anything. But she slept well that night and the next day she went on her usual morning walk with Papa. On his way to office, Papa dropped her at her school. "Study well. If you don't work hard you will not get admission into a good college." Florence did not go to college. She did not even seek admission to any college. They would not have admitted her even if she had tried. She joined St. Jude's Academy at the 'far end of Park Street to learn shorthand and typing, but ended up learning to operate the telephone switchboard. What would Papa have said to this? Florence was to have joined the Presidency College. She was to have studied for many years to be an engineer like her Papa, or to be a scientist. But her Papa's dreams lay buried, like Papa himself. In the soil of Chittaranjan.

The ambulance from the loco workshop is standing in the portico of their bungalow. Mummy is crying. "Is Papa dead, Mummy?" There is not a single tear in Florence's eyes. Papa's body lies covered with a sheet. There is a profusion of flowers in the room where Papa's body has been kept. Florence wants to have a glimpse of Papa. But that is not possible. It was a bad accident and his face has been disfigured beyond recognition. The room is full of railway officers. Their wives are consoling Mummy. Florence does not want to go near anyone. She cannot talk to anyone. She sits in the room where Papa is. Quietly, for many hours. Without crying. Her mind has no thoughts. Neither of the past, nor of the future, nor even of the present.

Every year Florence goes to Chittaranjan with Mummy. Before catching the train at Howrah, she visits New Market to buy fresh flowers that arrive every morning from Kalimpong. Florence no longer asks about the meaning of death. She knows. She now understands it so well. In the beginning, soon after they moved out of their bungalow at Chittaranjan for good and shifted to an Eliott Road flat in Calcutta, Florence had cried. She did not like the place at all. "Papa will not like this house. He would never come here." A long wait had neither changed the house nor brought her Papa home.

Thirteen years is not too young and Florence understands life much beyond her years. But what one understands in one's mind is yet so hard to accept internally. Silently, how many tears had she not shed in her mind even as her eyes remained dry.

Over the years, before the images in her memory had faded, how many times had she recalled so vividly that rain-filled morning when she had beseeched those people wearing black armbands who stood around the grave not to cover Papa with so much earth. It would be so difficult for him to come out. Papa never returned. Florence never went for a walk with Papa again. And now, even after understanding and accepting everything in the half awake moments of how many mornings had she heard the same voice, the same soft touch on her face, as if Papa was waking her up to come for a walk with him.

Florence got admission to the Loreto Convent at last. Poor Mummy! The world outside her home had been a closed book to her. And now she had to meet all sorts of people, make countless rounds. It was Mummy's ardent desire that Florence should go to the best school in town, that she should lack nothing. But there was no one to help her. Papa had never lived in Calcutta for any length of time. Mummy had belonged to Calcutta, but in 17 years of marriage, she had lost her contacts. And the whole environment was so different now. Papa was a proud man. He had lived aloof from his community.

His thinking was so different that he had made few friends and never cultivated his relatives. Mummy had not realized that admission to a good school was so difficult. Even the petty chores of everyday life had become impossible. Their entire way of life had suddenly changed so radically.

"Florence, I know Eliott Road is a typical Anglo-Indian area and you don't like it. I tried my best but they won't rent their houses to us." Florence knew that Mummy had tried so hard but no Bengali family would let their premises to an Anglo-Indian woman and her daughter. With the disappearance of Papa's protective wings, there was no escape from facing the bitter and harsh realities of life. In the Loreto Convent, there was no social bias but with every passing year, Florence had felt the social consequences of financial stringency. For the affluent, the condescending attitude towards the Anglo-Indian community was not so obvious. But its sharpness could not be ignored by the less prosperous. Still, Florence cannot forget her discussions with Papa, the attitudes inculcated in her by him.

The British High Commission had turned down Mummy's application for immigration to England. Two months later, the Australian High Commission did the same. Florence had also signed the application. She was prepared to do anything to please Mummy. But she had learnt that it was not so easy to please anyone.

"We don't belong anywhere, Florence", Mummy had said in despair. Poor Mummy! She cannot even understand that their applications were doomed from the start. Neither of them had any qualifications for finding any work abroad, and they would have become a liability for the government from the very first day of their arrival in the new country. Mummy had never visualized any need to take up any work outside her home. And now that her life-long dream of migrating from India was shattered, it was painful to pass each day with her sense of despair. In the face of constantly mounting costs, her savings and her husband's pension were proving woefully inadequate.

Three years have elapsed. It's a rainy day. Florence is going to Chittaranjan by train with Mummy. She keeps gazing at Mummy's face. The sky is overcast with dark clouds. It starts to drizzle and a thin spray of rain invades the compartment through the window. Florence longs to run into the open fields and get soaked in the rain. Mummy is 37 years old. How is she going to live her life? There is no dearth of sensible advice from people. "Dora, you must marry again." But at her age it is impossible to find a man like her first husband. And then there is Florence !... Will she be able to reconcile herself to another man in the house?

Florence had seen those bottles of brandy, brought stealthily into the house in the guise of medicines which emptied so fast. Once she had thrown all those bottles of 'medicine' out of the house. But Florence could not throw out the problem. Papa could have lived alone. But Mummy cannot. If Florence was not dependent on her, perhaps Mummy would have found a man. Some day Florence was bound to leave Mummy's house to make a life of her own. But, when? How? Where? As she sat watching the fleeting green fields out of the window of her fast running train, Florence could not find any answers.

"How beautiful you are?" How many times has the 17-year-old Florence heard these words. It's her last year at Loreto Convent. Florence has grown into a young woman, her body has filled out. A beautiful girl with a fine figure attracts so much attention. She cannot concentrate on her studies. The dreams of becoming an engineer or a scientist have faded. She searches for emotional stability, for an emotional centre to help her concentrate her energies. She is unable to share her thoughts and feelings with boys in her own age group. Pranab comes of an affluent family. She has driven to Diamond Harbour with him in his car. "At the party last evening all the boys were staring at you," he says. Florence is looking at the blue water of the river. Here the Hooghly assumes vast dimensions. Far away, a ship's black smoke spirals upwards against the grey sky. "They just couldn't take their eyes off you. I told them that you were an English girl on a visit to India." Pranab goes on. Florence withdraws into herself. She is unable to talk to him. On their way back, Pranab tries to kiss her. Florence is dismayed. What kind of game is this? For boys like Pranab, body play is an end in itself.

Now she knows. Girls like her will never be anything more than playthings in the lives of boys like Pranab. It will never be possible for the boys of his ilk to understand her or to share the conflicting pulls of her life. Their world was different. Florence cannot enter that world. She has to tread her path alone. There was no choice. Florence is overcome by weariness. A sense of despondency overwhelms her which even the quietude of the green paddy fields swaying in the breeze fails to dispel.

Florence is alone in her room. From her window she can see the hustle and bustle in the street below. Perhaps there is a procession passing along. The solitude of her room fills Florence with a sense of loneliness. She feels like going down into the street to join the procession. At least she would be in the midst of people.

Mummy wants to marry again. Florence had seen this coming for some time. That was why she had looked for a job and came to live in the YWCA hostel. She likes her job. The office has a clean and cheerful atmosphere. Getting lost in the mechanical routine of the office helps her forget her inner tensions. Mummy was never a regular church-goer. But for the past few months she has been going to the church meticulously every Sunday. She stays out for lunch and returns home late in the afternoon even as she knows that Florence must be waiting for her. Florence does not want to be a burden on Mummy. She wants Mummy to come to terms with her life in her own way.

After many years Mummy is taking an interest in her clothes and sprucing herself up carefully. When Florence returns from her office in the evening, she can smell the presence of a man in the house. There are cigarette stubs in ash trays. The glasses smell of whisky. Who could it be? Florence cannot conjure up a pleasant image. She knows the reality of their situation. Mummy never looks reality in the face, she just succumbs to it. Florence tries to understand. But she is young and cannot get over the idealism of her raw youth. Theoretically she is prepared to accept a man in place of Papa, but her heart rebels against the possibility and Mummy knows this so well. Yet she will go to the church on the day of Mummy's wedding. It is at St. Paul's Cathedral. She watches the bride alighting from the flower-bedecked car in a pristine white bridal dress escorted by a tall handsome man. As they walk down the aisle, people shower them with petals. But the man walking by her side is Robert. It is her own wedding day. Her images have overlapped. Perhaps because she does not wish to accept the reality of Mummy's wedding.

"Robert, you look so handsome. I am so proud of you," she wants to tell him. She wants to smile and talk to Robert. How many hours has he been sitting here? Not once did he leave the room.

He knows that Florence has reached the end of her road. Cover me well with earth, Robert! So that even my memories can't escape the grave. I can't bear to see you unhappy. Look it's raining again. You must not wear a black band. I do not like black. Put a big red rose on your lapel. In the end everything is decided in a single moment. Without much thought. And now it looks just like a game we play with ourselves. Nurse, give me the injection on the other side. Turn me over. I cannot bear any more injections on this side. But the nurse doesn't understand anything.

Robert has come to the YWCA hostel to fetch her. He is in his police uniform. How smart and elegant he looks! How many girls must have fallen for him. In the beginning, what stories had they told her about him? All lies! For, Robert has no eyes for anyone else. Robert has not even ever touched Florence. He knows how she dislikes the "YWCA girls night out aspect". And now they all admit that Robert doesn't even look at any other girl. He comes to see her so frequently. Always with such beautiful flowers! Seeing the blue police jeep, the *durban* of the YWCA hostel runs up to her room to inform her.

"Robert, next month I'll return to Mummy's house." Robert looks at her surprised. "Mummy's husband is migrating to Australia. He will send for her after a year. It is my last chance to spend some time with Mummy." Robert is driving the jeep. He does not say anything.

Night had descended. Yet the Strand is crowded. How many people have come to stroll along the bank of the Hooghly.

"Mummy says I should also apply for migration to Australia. They will sponsor my application. I am not qualified to work in an office. Mummy says that I have no future here."

Robert slows down the jeep. He looks at Florence intently. Then says, "And what about me?"

Florence slides across the seat and bending over the steering wheel kisses Robert on his lips. Robert stops the jeep and takes Florence in his arms, forgetting that he is in uniform and that his police jeep is standing in the midst of heavy traffic on the Strand.

Florence stayed in the Eliott Road flat with Mummy for only a few months. Mummy likes Robert. She has suggested that he should also migrate to Australia with them. Robert laughs it off. "If I had met you first, I would have married you," he says. "How would you have gone to Australia then?" Robert can please Mummy so easily.

Florence's marriage was performed by Mummy with great eclat. She loaded her with presents. Many people from Florence's office were present at the wedding and many officers from the police force were there. Das Babu did not go to work for three days. He had taken it upon himself to make all the arrangements for the wedding and had decorated the couple's new house himself. He had got Florence a special house rent allowance from the company. Only a clever man like him could have found such a nice house in a posh locality for such a small rent. The police department takes a long time in allotting houses to its officers. Besides, Das Babu knew that Florence would not like to live in the police colony.

And Das Babu has again taken it upon himself to make all the arrangements. He knew that Florence was hypersensitive. Even the smallest lapse would upset her. Das Babu has brought all the flowers this time. The company has extensive gardens filled with a large variety of flowers. Das Babu is fond of flowers. After the daily hassle and haggle with the union, it is flowers that help Das Babu keep his equilibrium. Every year the company bags a prize at the flower show of the Horticulture Society. Florence comes to the same garden with her lunch pack. Das Babu and Florence talk about flowers. This dried up old man, his mouth filled with *paan*, terror of the office, is an authority on flowers. How many books has he read, how many nurseries visited? Florence's wonder knows no bounds.

There was a lawn around each bungalow when she lived with Papa. Always, decked with flowers. Could the flowers bloom in the measly flower pots hanging in a small flat? But, why not? Das Babu replied, "You have only to be careful in tending the flower pots—the right amount of manure, sunlight and water according to the season." Das Babu longs for a daughter. A beautiful daughter—like the flowers. The very thought sends ripples through his heart. No no! It isn't done to let one's mind run berserk like this. It isn't graceful to impose oneself upon anyone. In his own way, Das Babu knows how to exercise self-control. After all, Das Babu is a self-proclaimed anti-social element! What hasn't he been through? What experience has he not had of the different facets of life? And now he wants a daughter! Das Babu has not had even a single *bira* of *paan* since morning.

There are dark clouds in the sky. A light rain begins to fall. And, then it stops. The prayer is being read. There are three shovels near the mound of earth. Robert is standing in front of the mound. His eyes are red. Perhaps, with grief, perhaps with crying. But eyes can get red for other reasons too—with the arrogance of his handsome looks, with pride in his uniform and his position in the police, and sometimes with whisky.

Florence dislikes liquor intensely. She has flung those bottles out of the window so many times. Come on Florence! Which policeman doesn't drink? Do you know what hazards we face on duty? Florence, you got so worked up over such a petty matter. It was only a small drink. That too, inside my own house. I had only asked my own wife to sit with me. Oh! what a child you are! Florence! Do you know sex is a big business? There were so many girls in that house. All of them are now in the lock-up. And what books did we find in that raid! I brought home just one magazine. Everyone enjoys these magazines. Come to me darling! Have a look! What fun these pictures are! Have a sip. And you got so offended over such trifles! Lost your temper completely, crying, "Chee! typical Anglo-Indian behaviour!" How could I not get angry? Bloody bitch, such superior airs! Always bloody Alice in Wonderland. Why did you keep answering back? You well knew that it was best to keep quiet. You knew how drunk I was. Did I slap her? Honestly. I cannot remember. I was too drunk. It had been such a long day. Robert had slept that night on a bench in front of the Victoria Memorial. For two days he could not muster courage to return home. "I was so ashamed. I could not bear to face you, Florence, my flower!"

Das Babu is looking for a *paan* shop. The afternoon is upon him. Meaningless end of a beautiful life! Every life is meaningless. But it's meant to be lived. Das Babu has not had his *paan* since morning. Everyone has gone. Only a small slab of stone remains to be installed. Of pure white marble. With "Florence" etched on it. And, on a line below it, yesterday's date.

***

The Homecoming

It had rained all evening. Ashok rose to leave when there was a break in the downpour but she kept him back on one pretext or the other. She was not sure if he understood, she was not even sure if she understood it herself. It had certainly not been planned that way.

The clouds gathered again and rain continued all night. She watched him listening to rainfall as he lay calm and peaceful after making love. She slept only in short stretches. They made love and held each other fervently all through the night. It was so different from anything she had known before. For no reason at all, lying next to him she felt so easy and comfortable, and a fragrant mood enveloped her in its warmth. She bent down and kissed him gently on the eyes as he lay asleep.

Surabhi lived independently in a small flat with a large terrace and a magnificent view of the beach with flocks of seagulls flying over its golden sands. She often held parties on moonlit nights on her terrace, and told her friends that it was excellent luck to have found the flat soon after she got her divorce. Gracefully draped in a silk sari, she entertained her guests including may visiting foreigners who were her friends from the years she had spent abroad.

Her Indian friends included many bohemian artists. They were happy to run errands for her because she invited them to elegant parties at her flat. And, also because she was unattached, attractive, and still quite young. She lived well without a regular job and they believed she was rich. They did not know that she supported herself through freelance journalism and frequent remittances from her father who had settled in Europe after Surabhi's mother died.

Surabhi came back to India on an idealistic impulse. Perhaps with a sense of nostalgia for the happy childhood she spent with her distinguished family of old lineage. She had wavered for many years before deciding to return. When she came finally, she was ready to settle down. After spending so many years abroad, she found it difficult to adjust to the conditions of life that she had lost touch with. She felt a sense of alienation in responding to people socially. There was a languorous quality to the atmosphere. Conversations lingered on and the words conveyed something quite different from the direct and clear messages that she was accustomed to in the West. But she resolved to stay in India. She married impulsively, without consulting her family, relying determinedly on the principle that her life was her own business.

The marriage turned out to be an experience she could have done without. She had presumed her husband to be what she wanted him to be. It had little to do with what he really was, which god alone knows is a complicated matter always. She herself, no matter how righteous she sounded, seemed to have little idea how she appeared to him. Human beings are like icebergs, she learnt painfully; what lies below the surface is far bigger than what you see above the water. For a length of time she endured her situation. It was hurt pride and a reluctance to admit that she had made a wrong choice. And then there was anger; the volatile efforts to force her husband to fit the image she had drawn to suit her wishful expectations. Divorce was a messy business with the tantrums she was shocked to find herself capable of.

It was a great relief to feel free after so much turmoil. She could do what she liked without the irritable omnipresence of a husband who left no doubts about his ownership rights to her body and soul. She could meet exciting people with a free mind, and her head swam with wonderful ideas which the pressures of marriage had put on the shelf. She met people, she liked, at a time and place she chose, without any bindings and compulsions of her married life. But the excitement wore off. Silently, the pressures returned—the old inner pressures which had led her to the marriage and settling down. There was a yearning again for the permanence of one relationship, for the secure feeling of finding the same familiar body touching hers as she lay awake in her bed when there was rain and thunder at night.

"You did really believe in the wonder that was India. Quite literally," Ashok said, the first time he was at a party at her flat.

"An excellent book," a foreigner interjected.

Surabhi looked across the table at Ashok. He was full of mischievous innuendos and was enjoying himself at the party. He had an inoffensive and a confident style. She wondered at his sense of ease in interacting with her foreign guests. She had noticed that it was difficult for most Indians who had not lived in the West to have a relaxed conversation with Europeans. Ashok was at perfect ease, lightheartedly discussing Krishna-Leela with her American friends.

"Krishna was a playful god."

"He liked women, especially other men's wives, like Raḍha," Ashok said.

They got on well from the start. Soon Surabhi thought they were in love, she seemed to know better what the word meant than him. She was an easier spirit. Her mind was not analytical like his and she tended to live more with the impulse of the moment. It was only after her marriage and divorce that she had begun to think about the mistakes she felt she had made with her life.

"She's got him all right, but what does she see in him?" her bohemian friends asked, angry to realize that they had failed to make the grade. Ashok was neither a bohemian, nor an artist. "What fun could he be for an intelligent woman?" Unlike them, who were mostly in love with themselves, he seemed normal. A bourgeois dilettante of sorts with a well-paid job. "Women are like that. No mistake the second time. She wants to settle down now with a safer man."

It surprised her indeed that he did not propose to her as she had expected. It was not that she cared for the legality, but she had thought that it was really she who had chosen him out of many, in a kind of modern day *Swayamvara*. Friendships were pleasant as they came, but she had looked for a deeper commitment. Ashok appeared keen enough, and she had no doubts about the sincerity of his attachment. And yet, she discovered that she wanted more than an open relationship. Strangely, it offended her to receive what she herself had so often offered to others, and what she believed to be the sane basis of a relationship.

Surabhi looked at herself in the mirror to see if there were any lines on her face. She took measures to check the firmness of her breasts. But the mirror reassured her. It could not be any of that. Ashok had always appeared so different from the men she had known before, but that had not bothered her earlier. Now, it intrigued her. It hurt her pride that she could not get what she wanted. It meant that she did not have sufficient power over him when almost absentmindedly she had believed that she could have him any time, even as it meant compromising her standards somewhat.

She must make it happen. It had never been necessary to plan such things before. They had always happened on their own. Reflecting over the situation, she realized that the best part of knowing him was that she felt so easy and comfortable with him. There was none of the tensions she had experienced with other men. And yet he was not dull—just a person to be with for short periods as she had earlier thought it to be.

"We must go out together more frequently," she decided.

They went out to concerts, plays, and social gatherings, but often he found convincing excuses to stay away. She discerned a pattern and realized that there was a kind of Lakshman-Rekha he would not cross. It was a line she could not draw in her mind's eye, and yet it existed. It was a fence which could not be crossed and which inexplicably kept a minimum distance in the midst of closest intimacies. It prevented any trespass into the inner privacy of his individual being.

She discovered that it was respect for the individual indemnity which gave the relationship a flavour she had not known before. It was as if their intimacy was constantly freshened by it, which could so easily have turned into a dull familiarity. It was amazing how one settled for dullness so easily, in marriage and out of it, and in so much else of life. Why did this happen? Was it fear, old age, physical infirmity or loneliness that crawled into the heart unwittingly as the years advanced. Did they compromise the standards one had upheld in the early years?

Stray whiffs of memory from her youth in the house of her grandparents made her think how she was forgetting the playful spirit or her childhood. None of the pleasures of adult life compensated for the loss of that joy. Could one not carry that playful spirit into the adult world of love-sex-work-relationships? Why must the loss be inevitable?

Surabhi remembered the emotional storms of her first love. With all its impracticalities and confusion, which were so transparent now, her heart still missed a beat when her thoughts turned to those moments. A pristine purity enveloped those moments. Why did emotions turn to a whining sentimentality in the mature years? Should the experience of passing years not give emotions a subtler, a finer, flavour?

Somewhere on the way to the practical world of adults, in learning the tricks to cope with adult life, she had lost the playful spirit of her childhood. Was it the first step into the descending stairwell of lost hopes and compromised standards, leading to an early old age, defeat and death, even when still far from the grave? Did it not happen if one learnt only to cope with the exhortations of the body, oblivious to the demands of emotions? Did she only pamper her body while her heart dried to the subtler shades of feelings, to the vibrant response of senses, to the magic of the world around her? How had she failed to realize that those vibrations of emotions ultimately shaped everything, even her body? She searched her heart. Her heart was still with her; she would search and shape it anew; she would defy fear.

"It is the suspense that keeps up my interest. He is smart and plays it well. And I had thought he was a simpleton." But she knew instinctively that no game was being played. It was just the way things were with him. She remembered the good and relaxed relationship that existed between her grandparents. Was that because of the distance they maintained? It was all so much in the past, in a different world. Were they playful? She knew so little of their inner lives. Could lives of a remote past have any relevance to the world she lived in?

Then, for the first time in her life she understood what love meant; that it was an unconditional affair; that she was only answerable to herself for the generosity of only her own feelings. Being in love was not a game of power any more. It was a reward in itself. Surabhi rejoiced in the moment not because she obliterated all thoughts of the future from her mind, but because she knew that if she lived joyfully that day, the future would take care of itself.

She looked at the flocks of seagulls flying over the blue waters of the bay. The monsoon sky was a riot of colours in the soft light of the evening. She sat on the terrace for a long time, watching the patterns clouds made in the evening sky. The gentle mood of the evening enveloped her completely. It was so far from the active and aggressive world she knew so well where good performance, even in love, was so important.

It was strange that without doing anything he was unlocking something inside her, enabling her to see herself in a clearer light. Why had she understood herself so little for all the years that she had spent doing things she never wanted to do? The things that brought her all the unhappiness and pain? What mysteries lay inside her? And what strength could she now discover in herself? Was that a gift of love?

"You should be careful," she was advised. "Men take advantage of a women so easily." Even her own mind had always reacted cautiously. "You should give only when you are sure to receive" was the caution which lay at the core, under all graces of her relationships.

How was it that she could trust him without any gnawing fear or anxiety, without that ever watchful eye on ensuring reciprocity which she had always believed to be her protection. She had switched off those early warning lights, demolished the radar itself, as if the enemy had a permanent change of heart. If losing did not bother you any more, what could you lose? And then she knew that it was the ever present fear of losing that had always made her a loser even when she had held all the winning cards. What could she finally win or lose anyway, except the peace in her heart?

The coming of that peace had taken a long time. It still came and went. Yet, now when she had tasted it, when she had felt it permeate deep into her head and heart, she knew that it would come again. She would make it come. She remembered the quarrels they had. The time they had returned to her flat after an outstation trip over the weekend.

"It was no fun. Everything in this country is so wretched and sloppy. You don't help. And now you want to get rid of me." She was tired and irritable, as she often was.

"You must be right. There is no need for anyone to suffer wretchedness. Applies to both of us." She was shocked when he got up and went away.

That was a long time ago when she had still not given up her efforts to fit Ashok into her image of him with the aggressive style she knew so well. When she still felt that her Western background naturally entitled her to her superior airs. Most people seemed to accept them so easily. It was the cult of Western superiority which, he said, the colonialists had injected so deeply and so systematically into the oriental psyche. The simple-minded drifted into it knowing no better. They basked in the reflected glory and the material advantages it brought; ignoring the psychic price they paid. They were oblivious to the conflicts they bred inside them through superimposing an attitude to life alien to their genes whose roots went back beyond even the generations of their great-grand-forefathers.

Was that the conflict which, unknown to herself, had ruined her marriage? Did she herself not believe, albeit unconsciously, that her upbringing and education in the West gave her an advantage even to know and admire India? It was only recently that she had begun to travel the long distance that lay beyond that naïve belief. It had nothing to do with superiority or inferiority, with the East or the West. It was the organic unity of her inner system from which she could not move away.

She had lived a long time in the vigorous West. She admired its courageous, if often aggressive, spirit which had eliminated so much physical misery from human life, which she was appalled to find everywhere in India. And yet, she reflected, perhaps the same aggressive spirit had turned on itself, weakening the traditional hold of humanity and reverence in the minds of men which was still a natural part of the ordinary people's lives in India. Untempered by humility and reverence, didn't the aggressive spirit of the West permeate the personal lives of its people? Did it not lurk just below the surface niceties, to inwardly corrupt the warmth and generosity of human relationships?

There was a lot of sentimentality in India which disgusted her. But now she was not sure if she would bargain this sloppily compassionate human warmth for the coldly correct behaviour of the West, for the loneliness which people tried to ward off mechanically. Did these things not change the inner elements of one's personality—from trust to suspicion, from a natural generosity to hard calculation, from the subtle play of emotions in one's heart to simplistic clinical attitudes? Did it not create a tension charged world, with little inner leisure?

Everything, even the human body, seemed to be in constant measurement on a scale of external perfection. Didn't it terrify people of old age? Did she not say to herself once in New York that she did not want to grow old there? Putting such a premium on the excellence of the physical aspects of life, didn't seem so realistic to her now. In India of the pot-bellied gods, even the artistic tradition subordinated the external form to manifest the beauty of the inner spirit, so notable classically in the superb Buddha images.

How had her impressionable years in the West affected her? How was one to know? The experience sank deep down, and yet rose to the surface instinctively to colour one's responses. Was one a prisoner of the conditioning? Of the *Samskaras*? Could all the education she acquired, which taught her to be clever and smart, not help in her emotional life?

She knew now that people had to struggle with themselves to find their freedom. Many tried, but for most it seemed a struggle that required more than a lifetime. What brought such success to only a few? It could not be the intellect alone. She had seen so many brilliant minds, so analytical and lucid in dealing with the external, and yet so distraught in their inner, personal lives. Was it a lack of compassion, the absence of that strange and yet so simple a word "love" that brought all that brilliance to nought when it came to what mattered the most?

"Free love must have come to Europe after central heating," Ashok once said. "You could not even see the human body properly in that cold weather, let alone revelling in it." They were on a visit to a medieval temple which stood out majestically above the flat plains. "In our climate, delighting in the human body must have come naturally to people, like arresting these *apsaras* in stone, permanently at eighteen."

She discovered strangely that the physical intimacies touched something deep in him which was not as she had originally thought, due to any inhibitions. His mind seemed to be involved in the act in an inexplicable manner. He seemed to enjoy the tension. And it was the lack of it which she liked. Perhaps it was this complementary quality which had built their relationship.

"How little I know him," she thought. But then, did it really matter? She had only recently begun to know herself better. If she did not even know herself, what chance did she have of knowing anyone else? And then, everyone changed with time and experience. How much had she changed herself? And this time, she was aware of it. Her body had become playful. Love, uncorrupted by the responsibility-reciprocity-obligation syndrome, was a pure joy that she revelled in. It did not bother her any more that her breasts would sag some day and her hips would lose their shape. Her body had acquired a resilience, her embrace an erotic warmth which she had not known before. Her body needed to be touched, to be played with, and all the juices surged through her body and heart, and her head stopped ticking all the time.

It was the warmth of their relationship which had opened out her inner life. She could say that now with ease as she rejoiced in the rich erotic ecstasy. It was the best things God ever created, she thought.

Surabhi was a spirited woman and wanted to be free and independent. She had braved man's world and had fought fiercely and then fear crept into her heart as she realized that a woman had to manufacture emotions, what else could she do? Only a man gave security. Didn't all the mothers teach this?

What was pleasure, and what did sex mean? She held out sex, the surest weapon a woman had to win. What else could she do when all the fruits of the earth were usurped by man? So she hung on to holding it back—tempting, promising, and denying, even as she longed for it herself. She mustered all his tricks, and fought, but she did not win. And then she relaxed and the fear was gone.

She then knew that it was not he who had changed her, even if she would have liked it that way. It was her own self which had changed her when she was ripe for a change. One changed with time, one's heart changed, one's needs changed. One had the possibility of changing all the time, for better or for worse. But Surabhi knew now that she could arrest herself to be the heavenly nymph if she could sustain her joy in the world she had found beyond the walls of reason. The mind may not help, but the gentle play of her heart would.

The Affair

As the first rays of the sun fell on the trees beyond the balcony the next morning and Suresh recalled everything, that the affair had really begun. More than anything else it was the fragrance which was not only perfume but something else too, more delicate and feminine than anything he had encountered before.

The shadows of tall buildings on the beach shortened as the sun rose. The city was gradually coming to life. He sat in a daze, his normally alert and analytical mind enveloped in a misty haze of mysteriously delicate smells and sensations.

It had all happened without his realizing what was happening, it was only much later that he understood that the flesh had a way of demolishing the brain. And he was glad to revel in the freer air of the senses, free from the bondage that the intellect had held him in for so many years after his wife had died.

Suresh had lived on his own for many years. That seemed to suit him best after those years of what he now called his child marriage. He remembered vividly the wedding which had taken place in a small town not far from where the first line of hills rose to meet the Himalayas. The ancient mansion was full of relatives and friends as the *barat* arrived with him on a splendid white charger. He had felt somewhat foolish climbing on to the horse, but his heart was full of excitement at the thought of a journey to regions whose mystery was to open out to him. He was embarking on the journey to full manhood, following the time-honoured custom of his ancestors.

"They make a fine couple," he had heard someone say as he was going round the *vedi* with his bride. The priest chanted *mantras*, but the only thing he understood of those ancient words was that it was to be a bond of friendship.

Both families had consulted match-makers and priests to settle the wedding. The young couple had met, but he did not know her; knowing was to begin after the wedding. He could not have said then, not even now after years of turmoil and thinking, whether it was good to have an arranged marriage. They had started on a clean slate, with a sense of finality to their commitment to each other. She had come to him young and as innocent as he was himself. Besides the *samskars* coming down from countless generations behind her, and some romantic ideas on love gleaned from the simple books which she had read, there was the inherent yearning for finding a permanence of happiness with him. The arranged marriage had saved them the turmoil of finding and judging, and they had started out with an easy heart to repose faith in each other. It was perhaps their innocent trust and faith which had evoked the best in both of them.

They barely had time to lose their innocence and wearing out the ecstasy of discovering the joy of the body before she died in childbirth. Later, as he often recalled, those joys of the body were so much purer, born as they were of the trustful abandon of their playful impulses. She died too soon to have known the inevitable turmoils of life. Too soon to have known whether she could have retained the fragrance of her innocence as years rolled by and events twisted the heart, and fear corrupted the faith she once had.

"She was the last of the innocents I knew," he always said of her. "Everyone I meet now seems so clever in comparison." But he also felt that the clever people he met were often so tense. Perhaps their ambitions outpaced what their systems could cope with.

He had also grown slowly in his awareness of the world around him, years behind most people he knew. It was not a bad thing he now understood. If the mysteries of the world unravelled slowly, one savoured the events. Experience had a deeper meaning if the flow of life was not forced and was permitted to run fast or slow at its own pace, It was better to let the experience seep in, and permit the system to respond from its depths.

"How would my life have been if she was alive?" The question had often tormented him. He dreamt of the idyllic life he had hoped to have. Memories of her kept him in a melancholic mood for a long time. But he had a strong will and his sense of life reasserted itself. His curiosity turned into a deeper quest for an understanding of the meaning of life. He was fond of travelling and visited many holy places, but religion left him dissatisfied. Though he liked the atmosphere of many ancient places of worship, the priestly discourses could not silence his analytical mind. He was unable to abandon himself to the unquestioning faith of any religious creed.

"Everything may not have worked out so well," he often mused as the years went by. "She may not have been able to cope with the turmoil of this rapidly changing world."

"Do you really think she was so helplessly innocent?" his friends asked.

"Her kind of innocence was too fragile," he replied. "The weight of traditions hung heavy on her. She would have withered if unforeseen events disturbed the set course of her life."

"Are you rebelling against the Indian traditions?"

"Not really, only that we need to burn a lot of deadwood. With modern physics describing matter as a manifestation of consciousness, it would be foolish to abandon the Upanishads. To grasp the ancient wisdom one needs a deep mind. Faith is different, it is easier; our lives would be happier if we could find faith."

"Do you aim to renounce the material would for spiritual uplift, for a purer spirit?"

"Have a whisky. It's good spirit," someone else quipped.

Years had gone by. Suresh had risen in his career. But he had never ceased to be amazed at the barren emotional lives of the so-called successful people. They invariably crossed the threshold of a rising career before reaching the middle years of life. It was a like an aeroplane breaking the sound barrier. Their mental faculties took a firmer shape through the experience they absorbed. However, their freedom of spirit to venture into new areas of exploration remained limited to the areas of the physical and material world.

Suresh wondered why the qualities of their mind did not operate in their inner lives. The external efficiency seemed to feed on their emotional system. But didn't the quality of emotional life affect the intellect, even the body, deeply? Could one remain intoxicated with success so completely as to obliterate or weaken the emotional calls? When one lay down in bed at night, peeled off all the masks, shelved the tricks, and was entirely and helplessly into his own self, didn't sadness crawl into the heart?

It was the same situation for both men and women he thought. Only the externals were different. Men controlled wealth, wielded power, and could confer privilege. Women, knowing no better, used their sex to short-change men where they were vulnerable. It was a war fought with different weapons, with an ever elusive victory for either. The odds were against women; their weapons had only a few years of use, and would not fire the same arrows with all the fiery cosmetics of the world.

"What a marvellous view you have of the sea," Suresh said. He had met Divya at the house of a common friend. Later, she had invited him to a party at her flat which overlooked a long stretch of the beach. The friend had told him admiringly about her courage in facing a rather messy divorce. Standing next to her on the terrace, he felt the proximity of her well-proportioned body, and said, "Some people receive all the blessings from God without even asking."

She was an attractive woman conscious of the impact she made on men. She turned to him with a charming smile. "I worship a female deity who is kinder than all the male gods."

He liked the way she spoke. She did not have the blunt edges of a feminist. There was an air of courage and spirit about her which appealed to him. With all the scars of a bad marriage and the trauma of a divorce behind her, she was a breath of fresh air compared to the single women he had met. There was always something sad about the women of that age not engaged in the ultimate womanly profession of marriage. They were either resigned or too eager. Marriage, a man, is the core of achievement. For centuries the women had it drummed deep into their very genes.

At social gatherings, the women rarely made much impression on him. The married women exuded an air of complacency. Young girls looked frivolous, and did not attract him despite the freshness of their young bodies. The mature single women were rarely invited; they threatened the secure world of marital bliss, re-kindling the burnt-out fire in the loins of aging men bored with their monogamous lives. Spinsters, stuck with their virginity, did not know the tricks; they had never made it to the good game. Divorcees promised the spice. They had tasted the fruit. They were the feared poachers of the reserved forests.

"Ninety per cent of men think about women ninety per cent of the time," he had heard a modern-day guru exhort his disciples. "If you deny yourself the joys of the body, the hunger will always trouble you."

Suresh could not have denied his longing for the soft warmth of a woman's body. It was an erotic desire, and much more. It was a need for touch, for the unspoken communication, for finding the emotional balance. It was a need to find faith, to create trust, and to share not only the body. Yet he was afraid. He had lost his courage and was lost in the search. It was easier when one was younger. Then it was almost an in-built process of growing up. One risked instinctively and knew, even without understanding it, that courage was the only security one could ever have.

Suresh got on well with Divya from the start. He was surprised himself. They had such different interests and backgrounds. Divya had an incredible amount of energy which he admired. He often wondered what went on in her head to generate so much activity. She got involved in so many things and met several people who were drawn to her not only because she was an attractive single woman, but also because she had a sharp intelligence and was competent at her work. And yet, she arranged to spend time with him by herself when she discovered that he did not enjoy company.

"You are so unsocial and phlegmatic," she told him, "I wonder how you get on so well at work.

"Wisdom, dear Divya," he opened the book he was carrying. "The elephant is the wisest of animals, he moves slowly and often stays completely still for long periods," he quoted. And then he added, "Restless activity is only for those who lack sound judgement."

"For all your wisdom, you are so lonesome," her voice floated in from the veranda teasingly. But there was affection in it. "With such good judgement why couldn't you find yourself a wife in ten years?"

"With your kind of energy, I would have a harem by now," he said, "You are not doing badly though. Why don't you set yourself up as a courtesan? You would be a great hit."

"Even courtesans have their favourites," she teased him again, "at least for short periods."

He could not deny that he had been lonesome. He had learned to live with his books and other interests. Could they really be a substitute for human relationships? But his fears always returned. How could you know a human being? There was so much that lay so deep within them. Intelligent people learned to wear their masks so well. Lacking faith, there was no way of coping with what really went on inside them. In a crisis, the masks came off and horrors bubbled forth. The memory box played back scenes from the remote past with high fidelity. His observations over the years had driven him back to himself, repeatedly.

"He thinks too much." Divya sat looking at him. She was happy to be with him. She felt so easy and relaxed, even frivolously mischievous. She had found faith, and could trust him instinctively.

Suresh did not believe that she wanted to possess him. An intelligent woman did not indulge in such things, neither by aggression nor by becoming a door mat. Could she be thinking of such things? But she was not given to much introspection. Perhaps she had not even thought silently within herself why her marriage had not worked. Perhaps she knew by experience that human life had a rhythm of its own which could not be altered by deliberate effort.

She was an ambitious woman, even if she did not clearly know the direction to realize her ambitions. Perhaps it was her thwarted ambitions which had often made her so angry in the past, she had told Suresh.

"Lack of love and emotional imbalance lead to ambition," Suresh said.

"You are not getting much love yourself." Divya had smiled mischievously.

How did she understand love? Suresh had wondered. It was nice to love, to be loved, and not only physically which certainly was nice. Was love, like so much else of life, a mere chance circumstance? Did we react instinctively to the object of love, or was it a deliberate effort? And how could you ignore the compulsions of physical existence which made you see things in light of your need for them?

She had learnt to control her temper by the sheer need to cope with the practicalities of life. There was no longer a husband to smoothen out the effects of a tantrum. Unless she controlled herself, the maid did not stay to cook the food or wash the linen. The compulsions of day-to-day living had forced her to know better.

Suresh realized that even he was a practical need. She could not have denied it. It was the same all over the world. She must have learnt that it was a man's world even as she had spent many years in fancy schools and universities of America where everyone swore by equal rights. And now, after the divorce and with the advancing years, she must know that despite the economic freedom and her fine career, a woman still wanted a man. And, didn't he want a woman even though all the servants in the world took care of his house, and the whores of the world, his body?

"Men are so clever. They have even manipulated language in their favour," Divya said, "In a relationship a woman is either a wife or a mistress. But the man is the master even when not a husband. Master is the only available word."

"The clever will always dominate the ignorant. But generosity is possible sometimes." It was Suresh's turn to tease her.

She refused to be baited. "Men pamper a woman with small tricks like opening doors for her, and gifting items of jewellery. But they dominate her in every real sense. A woman is conditioned to believe that she is not made for the difficult things which only men can do."

"But women can do all the things men do. Even do them better. It is the men who cannot accomplish so many things which are possible only with a feminine temperament."

"Of course, yes," she said, "Women are the self-sacrificing comforters, loving mothers, forgiving wives, ultimate givers of unbounded love. Men wisely decide not to be capable of such accomplishments. Behind every man lies a sacrificed woman."

Suresh looked at her quizzically and said, "The further behind she is the better."

She was not the sacrificing kind. Her experience and ambitions prevented such emotional recesses of the heart from overwhelming her. She believed that if one wanted a place in the world, a certain kind of determination, even ruthlessness, was unavoidable. Nothing could be achieved if one frittered away one's energies in sentimental dreams. And yet, she had now begun to pause to ask what did such concentration of energy achieve finally if one never tasted the joy of caring as simply as the autumn leaves rustle in the breeze? She wondered sometimes about the success she had been looking for, which by its nature polluted the joy she now experienced in her life.

He looked at her quietly. She seemed angry. Something must have happened at work. She was an attractive and intelligent woman. The combination made her life difficult. Beauty may not always bring arrogance but it so easily took away humility; intelligence brought ambition which fostered an aggressive spirit. She would rise higher if she learnt to climb on the backs of others. Clever ones could do it almost gracefully. There were no easy paths to success in a man's world. And men could tolerate, even admire, a woman who had beauty or intelligence, but not a woman who had both.

"Beauty provokes desire. And an intelligent woman ensures that you pay the price. No short-changing the clever girl." He remembered what a friend had once told him. "Women learn the worth of their curves quite early. The smart ones preserve their treasures for the best bidders. Women have tricked men on chastity. Men don't need it. Women do."

He looked at her again. Why didn't he marry her? He was free. And now that she had known him for a long time, she might want to seal the relationship, to give it permanency. Did she feel this at all? How could he be sure? Didn't everyone long for permanency of things they liked? But nothing was permanent no matter how much you wanted it to be. Didn't he want permanence? Permanence of her presence, of her playful laughter, of the fragrance of her smile, of the way she looked at him, of the feelings she stirred in his heart by just being somewhere in the world. How could he make all this permanent? Could anyone put a seal on such permanence?

They had a free relationship. And the fragrance came from that freedom. And then, one wanted to encroach on the freedom out of fear, and one lost the fragrance. One could not find the strength to live with the fragrance for long. One loved it too much and wanted it secured and sealed permanently, not realizing that the very attempts at permanence froze the poignance of emotions. What did a body matter when the spirit's fragrance had left it? It could only corrupt and decay, Corruption was so easy.

"Why don't you marry her?" his friends asked. "She will make you a fine wife. Don't you want to settle down? You two will get on like a house on fire. What will you do with your freedom when you are old with no one to look after you?"

"I will get a nurse," he said. "Besides, I don't like the word spouse. It rhymes with mouse."

But freedom was not a prize in itself. And why should a relationship diminish freedom and not refine it? Marriages are so unpredictable. So easily they become a relationship of possession, ownership, and coercion. A wife, or a husband, becomes an extension of one's personality, reflecting the quality of one's choice, enforcing an expected standard of behaviour.

He did not like to measure up to anyone else's standards. Her image of a husband would compel him to conform to her expectations of behaviour. And this had germs of conflict. Why should one invite conflicts? It would be delightful to have her all to himself in a passionate, exclusive possession. But how did tomorrow look? How did it all weigh in the balance? And what did she think of it?

She was a fine woman. He had never met anyone who fitted better in his image of a woman. She fitted so well on the pedestal he had made for her. One could draw any images in one's heart when one was fond of a person. Did she like the pedestal? And what of the pedestal she may have for him? Pedestals were difficult things. One could lose one's balance so easily to fall and break. There was too much strain in balancing on a pedestal. It corrupted one's inner mechanism. External pressure, especially when an emotional attachment lent it a greater power, distorted one's view of the world. The discord would appear on the face. And that would not do.

He watched her as she came in through the open door. He liked the flowers she wore in her hair. The sun had set, and he watched her sari fluttering in the breeze. Soon it would be dark. He wanted to hold her. Would she ask him to hold her? It would be good to hold her anyway.

In Retrospect

He woke up late. It was a Sunday morning. Rays of morning sun filtered into the room through the window. The week did not seem to have really gone by and Monday appeared only a distant probability. How long ago was it when he saw the sun's rays playing on Amaltas leaves? For many days now, forty-five years-old Subhash Narain Kaul had lost control of his memory.

Last week he had gone to register an urgent letter at the GPO and forgot his car keys at the counter. After searching everywhere in the car and reprimanding his two children sitting in the car for meddling with his keys, when he finally returned to the counter, he could not remember the number of keys in the bunch.

"It is strange. Imagine not knowing the number of keys in your own key ring," the counter clerk regarded him with disbelief.

A few days ago a friend had telephoned him, "You forgot your daughter in our house."

He had gone to his friend's house to discuss a matter and had taken his young daughter along for the car ride. After his discussions he returned home alone, forgetting all about the girl who was playing in the garden with other children.

Pramila, his wife of twelve years, had looked at him with great amazement.

Beyond the window, branches of Amaltas trees swayed in the breeze. He remembered the rows of Amaltas and Gulmohar trees in his college. Why were the twenty-five-year old memories of red and yellow blossoms flooding his mind for the past few days?

"What is so interesting outside the window?" his wife asked as she brought the morning paper and a cup of tea.

"I had a strange dream last night," Subhash said. "I was in an aeroplane which was flying at a great height above the clouds. The sky was a deep blue, and below me, thick clouds shone in the brilliant light of the morning sun. Then it occurred to me that they were not clouds but snow fields high up in the Himalayas."

"Your imagination is really running wild." Pramila was in a hurry to go back to the children's room.

Subhash could not finish telling her that he had opened the aeroplane's door to step out in the snow field. The snow was soft and fluffy, and as he went towards the high mountain peaks, he fell into a crevasse. Falling through the icy walls of the crevasse, he saw that the mist had returned. And then he was floating in a blue sky under the dazzling white of a fully opened parachute.

"Dreams have a relation to reality," he had read somewhere. But for a long time now he had given up the effort of going deep into anything beyond the affairs of his office. Success in one direction should be enough for a man.

The cane sofa set was enamel-painted last week. Blue cushions stood out brilliantly against its white paint. New curtains of a maroon Rajasthani print had recently been hung in the drawing room.

"There can be no doubt that Pramila's refined taste stands far above the level of the wives of my colleagues," Subhash thought, as he was shaving in the orderly neatness of a well-appointed bathroom. Pramila's choice of furniture and other household effects was a matter of envy for his friends. Subhash had not forgotten the change that had come into his life in the last twelve years of marriage. But now, for many days, his memory had run adrift. He often forgot things he needed to remember, and many unconnected things needlessly floated into his mind.

As he continued shaving, he looked at the greying hair on his head reflected in the mirror. He recalled Mr. Sahai, his colleague in office, who dyed his hair every Sunday.

"A young Mr. Sahai reaches the gates of old age by Saturday," Subhash often teased him. Pramila did not have a trace of grey hair.

"Papa! Papa! Papa!" Four-year-old Malu came running into the bathroom. "What are you doing, Papa?"

The younger of his two children, little Malu was Subhash's favourite. Ten-year-old Ravi was born soon after their marriage. Subhash did not want any children in the first few years of marriage. Perhaps in those early days, Pramila and he could have transformed their acquaintance into an intimacy if they were not burdened with child-care. But that did not happen and thoughts of what might have been had lingered on with him.

On Sundays breakfast was at ten, one hour behind the normal schedule. Across the sparkling black mahogany table, Pramila was pouring milk into a blue glass tumbler for Malu.

"Only seven of the twelve tumblers have survived," Pramila said. "Our servants have no sense of working properly." Her open tresses flowed over her housecoat to reach below the cushion of her chair. Her face, without any make-up, was still heavy from the slumber of a late morning sleep. Pramila never used any makeup. Perhaps it was this that had primarily attracted him to her twelve years ago.

Looking across the table, Subhash remembered that Pramila's face resembled the features of a girl who was a fellow student with him in college. It was an old story now. But in the initial years of marriage, Pramila had felt that besides physical resemblance, Subhash had also looked for many other parallel responses. Pramila did not like it and Subhash never found those responses. But, with the passing years they had forgotten all about it.

Ravi was tall for his ten years. Pramila had registered his name in a highly prestigious public school long before he was borne. He was due to join the school as a boarder in a few months. But neither of them cared to register Malu's name in any school. Pramila perhaps did not attach the same importance to girl's education. And Subhash's inaction had an element of escaping the unpleasant possibility of Malu's absence from home.

At twelve, Mr. and Mrs. Mani came to call on them with their seven-year-old daughter.

"You did the right thing," Mrs. Mani said. "Our child was offered admission in a top-of-the-line school in Ooty but I refused to send her. I was in that school myself as a child. But even the old schools have turned topsy-turvy these days. Children get completely out of control in boarding houses. It is best to keep the girls at home."

Looking at her, Subhash remembered that Mrs.Mani always bought clothes from a famous shop in London which specialized in children's clothes. Besides the convenience of ready-made good taste, which eliminated the risk of making a wrong personal choice, those outfits had a clear stamp of high price. It was impossible not to know the high standard of life of the Mani family from the children' attire.

In his childhood, Subhash went to an ordinary school of the small town his parents lived in. Fate had helped him, besides his own efforts, in rising above the limitations of his early life. Later, it was Pramila who raised their family life to a high social level. He overtook many of his colleagues on that basis alone. But well before meeting Pramila, he had already achieved a high status in his work without which marriage with Pramila would not have been possible. Conflicting pulls in his mind of different choices had finally resolved into a single direction. The lingering doubts about the choice he had made gradually dissipated in the flow of the passing successful years.

"Ravi will go to a boarding house in a few months," Pramila was proudly informing her guests.

"Where did I read that Indian public schools have failed to produce a single student of distinction in any creative field?" Subhash said. He was opening beer bottles.

Pramila looked at him in alarm. In the early years she had often wondered if she had made the right choice in marriage. But that was a long time ago, and now when life flowed with the security of a high level pattern she had known from her childhood, why was Subhash breaking off into such absurdities so often now? Pramila could not understand what Subhash could complain about.

"Most Generals of the Indian Army come from public schools," Mani countered in his restrained soft accent.

"Creative contribution does not mean perpetuating the beaten bureaucratic tracks in public offices or private industry." Subhash wanted to burst out: "Is there a single scientist, artist, musician, writer or politician who is the product of these schools?" But he restrained himself and wondered how such a thought had occurred to him.

"I meant that standards in our public schools have fallen very sharply," he said apologetically.

"I was just suggesting to Pramila that she should have a governess to teach Malu at home," Mrs. Mani said in relief.

Pramila accepted the suggestion half-heartedly. Perhaps there was an unconscious effort in it to ward off the developing emptiness of the coming years. Subhash had observed in the last few months that Pramila was losing interest in the Ladies Social group and the Sangeet Sabha. She still participated in their activities, but with a constantly neutral, inanimate expression enveloping her face. Subhash often wondered why for a long time now he had not seen Pramila's face radiating with a sense of enthusiasm and inner happiness.

"Any definite news of Rooney's return to London?" Mani enquired.

Subhash's office colleagues and their wives believed that he would take charge of the company when the existing boss Rooney returned to London. His friends were envious of his continuous rise. It was perhaps for this reason that many of his snooty colleagues overlooked the class deficiencies in his mannerisms. Years ago, Subhash had felt that his marital stability also depended on his ability to remain at the top of the race. But he was now used to remaining ahead by channelizing all his energies in a single direction. But strangely now, at the last rung of the ladder, his mind was often flooded with the dreams of his early youth. For some time now when he lay awake in early mornings and looked at Pramila's sleeping face, he tried to remember where he had seen it before.

"Nothing is decided yet," Subhash replied.

Pramila and Mrs. Mani looked at him in disbelief. Subhash knew that at his level, confidential matters had to remain confidential till the very end. His personal life and the office were two separate spheres which could not intermingle. But for the past few months he had begun to feel that this was not so. Perhaps his life at home and in office was part of the same pattern. It was a single quality that shaped his life in the office and with his family.

"Papa, I am going to a fancy dress party in flat number four," Ravi announced at the lunch table. "Mummy said I can be a policeman."

"Papa! Papa! I also want to go," Malu climbed off her chair and crawled under the table towards him.

"Get out of there, Malu! What nonsense is this?" Pramila suddenly flared up. "Ayah, take her away to eat in the children's room."

Above the violet blouse and the pink organdie sari, the tension on Pramila's face was not entirely on account of Malu. Amidst the neat rows of unread books in the detergent-cleaned sparkle of her house, a probability of disturbance in the predetermined order had shaken her balance. But after so many years of success and prosperity there was no longer any question of insecurity of a material kind.

Innumerable Sunday afternoons had passed in the slumber of beer bottles. Pramila was fast asleep under the cool air of the air conditioner. Her clear skin and firm body reflected only the first traces of passing youth. Brought up in the security of a predetermined social order, Pramila had known moments of doubt only in the first few years of life with Subhash. But for the last few days, a sense of inability to cope with the unfamiliar pressures coming from beyond her limited world, often led to helpless outbursts.

"Malu, you walk behind me." Both children were waving flags in the drawing room with handkerchiefs tied to a long stick in their hands. They were shouting "Zindabad ! Zindabad !", copying the processions on the streets.

Little Malu took his affection for granted. But Ravi was hesitant in his approach to him. The open-hearted laughter of a self-assured Malu was of a different quality from Ravi's unsure strains. Perhaps an easy sense of security and affection from birth, had allowed little Malu to look at the world always with her happy and trusting eyes.

The first few years after Ravi's birth were strenuous in the married life of Pramila and Subhash. They never developed an inner intimacy. In the later years they had externalized their aspirations and set limits to their personal relationship. But in those years, Subhash had not left his days of carrying the red flag of the Students' Federation so far behind. In contrast to most of his left wing colleagues in the Students' Federation who did not rise much above a clerical level, perhaps he alone had achieved a high level of material success. He no longer had any connection with the left wing, or with any other wing. What happened to those dreams of a country-wide revolution, and building a new society? But how could he now know the quality of lives of his friends of those days?

"Driver! I'he children are messing up the drawing room. Tell the ayah to take them for a drive."

The sky was full of clouds. He did not feel like going out. Now he could not sleep on many Sunday afternoons. Perhaps it was the uncontrollable lure of indulging in his daydreams of long forgotten past years that kept him awake.

Fresh garlands covered the photograph of Baba Ramdas on the mantelpiece. A few months ago, a friend from the Ladies Social Group had persuaded Pramila to join Babaji's gatherings. Then, Subbulakshimi's recordings of Meera's Bhajans came to the house. And for the first time, story books connected with the Ramayan and Mahabharat appeared in the children's room along with European comics. Subhash remembered the books he had read as a child. His father had kept a strict watch on the books he read. Many times his ears were boxed on discovery of unacceptable books.

In the activity-filled world of today, how could one possibly find free time? It was as if twenty-four hours of the day had shrunk to twelve hours. But he found it surprising that till recently, in spite of the usual routine of beer, club, and cards, he found many Sundays interminably long.

For the past few months, since he was told that Rooney would soon hand over charge to him and go back to London, his mind was often filled with a sense of meaninglessness.

"Formless and without attributes, or with a full form and many attributes," Subhash had decided to attend Babaji's prayer meeting a few days ago. Pramila was surprised beyond words. "Look for light, act, and have faith. The end is the same. Know your limitations. Know your inner self."

Thirty years ago his mother chanted prayers every evening in the puja room upstairs. He remembered parts of the Gayatri Mantra even now. The image of his mother through the rising smoke and fragrance of *Samagri* often came to his mind.

After many years, curiosity about a religious gathering had drawn him to Babaji's prayer meeting where women outnumbered men. Till a few years ago, he could not even have dreamt of finding Pramila in such a place. He liked the open-hearted, child-like laughter of the seventy-five-year-old Baba. The laughter dazzled through the gathered forms in the meeting, beset with advancing years and slowing minds. It was, as if that laughter signified a ray of hope and peace for those directionless souls.

"Religion is the opium of the masses," he remembered his own words at a meeting of the Students' Federation a long time ago. Why do those words of a long-forgotten past float into his mind now? He had not visited any temples or religious sites in the last thirty years, except for their archaeological ruins. Pramila and he did not observe any religious rituals on the births of Ravi and Malu. He had written in his will, now safely deposited with his solicitors, that after his death his body should be cremated without any religious rites. But he liked Babaji's laughter.

"Good night, papa," Malu said, putting both her little arms around his neck. Ravi said good night, standing at a distance.

One day Ravi had also attempted putting his arms around him. But the awkward unfamiliarity of the act had embarrassed both of them. Closeness was not easily possible. The population of the world had doubled in the last forty years. On this basis, loneliness should have halved. But why does it keep increasing? What has gone wrong with the order of life?

Pramila had gone to attend a music festival organized by the Sangeet Sabha. After dining alone, he was strolling on the lawn. Beyond the neutral shadows of Amaltas trees the fragrance of Rajnigandha filled the night.

The headlights of Pramila's car returning from the music festival lit up the trees lining the driveway. In the first years of marriage they used to go to the cinema several times a week, perhaps to escape the conflict between Pramila's extrovert personality and Subhash's introspective nature through external excitement. The curiosity of a young marriage and the attractions of sex were with them. The excitement of days of intimacies with Pramila had then mellowed in the routine of everyday life.

Traditional pressures for the stability of family had prevented dissolution of their marriage during the difficult days after Ravi's birth. Sexual attraction had dominated their married life in its initial years. But amidst those satisfactions, they had failed to forge any deeper unity in their lives. And then, they had slowly drifted into their individual ways with a dispassionate neutrality.

"Pramila! Pramila!" She had dropped off to sleep in the cool comfort of the air conditioner. He switched off the bedside table lamp, and looked at the moonlight on Amaltas branches outside the window.

"Pramila! Pramila!" he said as he lifted the sheets to get into bed. Pramila murmured something and shifted to rest her head on his shoulder. Her firm breasts still exerted a pleasing pressure on his chest. She had not breast-fed her two children. She did everything to maintain the firmness of her body, just as he had done everything to achieve success.

Subhash's decisive world did not have shades of grey between the sharp edges of black and white. And now, in close proximity of the summit, why was he turning inwards to enter that vast expanse of the grey land? Perhaps the essence of life was beyond the boundaries of black and white. Perhaps it was in that grey region whose unending vibrations had moved away from his life.

"How are dreams formed and how do they affect us?" he thought. He had got used to taking decisions with full control of the situation. He had shaped his life with an iron will. It would not be fair now to transfer the blame to anyone else. In the deepening night he could feel the warm proximity of Pramila's body. Why had these images and dreams not interfered with his life before?

At seven-thirty the next morning when his bearer bought the tea-tray and the newspaper, Subhash Narain Kaul's uncontrolled memory could not recall his dreams and thoughts of the night.

The Siberian Crane

Two years ago, I was spending my summer months in a house I had built in the high ranges of Himalayas. The land for the house on a hilltop was found by my friend Shailendra who ran a hotel in a neighbouring town. Later, a year after my house was ready, he also built a guesthouse in the middle of a forest some distance away from my house.

It was at his guesthouse that I first met Maria and Svetlana. I had gone there to invite Shailendra to a party at my house that evening. I was also curious to see the much talked about forest guesthouse, which attracted many foreigners trekking to the high mountains and glaciers. They apparently liked the place so much that they were willing to spend a day or two in the tents that Shailendra set up for them inside the compound when regular rooms were not available.

The footpath to the guesthouse led from the main road and it soon descended into a dense oak forest. I was struck by the number of small streams emerging from the mountainside, which glistened in the rays of the morning sun filtering through the trees. Shailendra had really discovered an amazing place for his guesthouse.

I found him sipping tea, sitting leisurely on a small platform near a cluster of trees close to the two-storeyed building of the guesthouse. Maria and Svetlana sat around a table in front of the platform, basking in the warmth of the morning sun.

Shailendra introduced them, "They have come to India to escape the Russian winter. Svetlana runs a business of her own in Siberia, and Maria is a teacher at a school in Moscow."

It was eleven in the morning. The sky was a clear blue above the greenery of the forest. Fluffy, cotton-like clouds floated lazily in the sky. The chill in the morning air was getting warmer with the rising sun. As I pulled a chair to sit down, a cat leapt out of the bushes to climb the platform and looked curiously at us.

Maria smiled at me and attempted a conversation in her broken Hindi, "Moscow had early snow this year. In the last week of October when I opened my window in the morning, I saw the lawn, trees, and rooftops shrouded in a thick, white blanket of snow. Perhaps, the snowfall had started after midnight."

"Oh! So you have learnt a smattering of Hindi?" I exclaimed in surprise. "But if you are more comfortable with English, I wouldn't mind it."

"The other lady, Svetlana, speaks neither English nor Hindi," Shailendra said. "But she is a smart one. Without any knowledge of Hindi or English, she managed the trip to India on her own, including two weeks in Goa. She met Maria in Delhi, who now interprets for her. Maria has many interesting stories about Svetlana's adventurous life."

Svetlana's countenance spoke for itself. She looked clever and smart, had a beautiful figure and was fully conscious of the impact she made on men. Dressed all in black with a trendy feminine black hat, she wore a thin black veil covering her ears, eyes, and partially her nose. High-heeled stilettos were an invariable part of her elegant, alluring style.

"The beautiful lady in black with her come hither glances, exudes a mysterious charm, which creates turbulence in men's hearts. She seems to know perfectly well that no man can resist her if she decides to reach out to him," Shailendra said about her. And, he continued to say so for many days even after she left for Delhi on her way back to Russia.

Maria said that both of them were going out for a walk in the surrounding area. "Svetlana likes this forest. She says that unlike the forests in cold countries, these trees are full of fragrance because of the strong sun. She wants to pack our lunch and walk aimlessly through the forest for a few hours, to get a feel of the woods. I just don't understand her ways and always wonder about the crazy ideas she comes up with."

"Just look at the fancy shoes of our lady," remarked Shailendra, "She won't change them even for walking in the forest. But I can't say anything because wearing the same shoes she literally runs up the scraggy pathway to the main road without blinking an eyelid."

Shailendra came to my house that evening accompanied by Svetlana and Maria. Most of the guests had already arrived. It was still an hour for the sun to go down. Svetlana, with her style and gestures, became the centre of attraction in no time. There seemed to be a craze to photograph her – in the front lawn and under the trees in the garden. She was really very photogenic and happily she continued to oblige everyone with charming smiles and poses in her carefree manner. She looked every inch a bold and spirited woman, proud of her looks. Her ability to bring varying expressions to her face was astonishing.

Looking at the photo-session, a friend—a movie-buff—remarked, "This lady reminds me of a film of the Italian director, Fellini. The mysterious heroine of that film was also dressed in black with a similar veil. She, like the lady here, had a manner of conveying a lot without uttering a single word. Just look at the style; this lady has all it takes to play the lead role in a film."

But Maria had an altogether different style. Their outlook on life and temperaments also seemed poles apart. Svetlana dressed stylishly, while Maria was content to be in a plain shirt and a pair of jeans with a plain yellow shawl covering her shoulders. One was bold and blithe, while the other was shy and simple. It occurred to me that perhaps it was these differences that had attracted them to each other.

As Shailendra and I wandered in my garden, he said, "There are some good flowers here. If you are open to giving me a few saplings, I will send my gardener to collect them. We have many sunny spaces in front of our rooms. These flowers will bloom so well there."

Then, watching Svetlana holding forth under a rhododendron tree full of bright red flowers, he said, "She is a crazy woman. This morning, when I looked out of the window from my room, I saw her lying down on the platform just in her bra and panties, enjoying a sunbath. The waiter carrying a tray of tea for her was so scandalized by the open display of her body that he left the tray quickly and fled from the scene."

Shailendra was quiet for a moment. Then he said, "So many foreign women have stayed at my guesthouse, but I never met anyone like her. I am surprised that as a mother of a twelve-year-old girl and running a successful business all on her own, she can be so free-spirited. She is undoubtedly a gutsy woman. Sometimes I think she is just a wild and superficial woman. But then, perhaps some deep-rooted experiences lie behind the facade of her free style."

Shailendra's gardener arrived the next day to collect the saplings. It was past eleven o'clock. As I went to the garden, I was surprised to find that Maria had accompanied him. She was wearing the same blue jeans, white shirt, and the yellow shawl.

She flashed me a smile and said, "My apologies for coming uninvited."

Then, bending down to the flowerbed, she said, "These flowers smell so nice. They are small in size compared to the ones we have in Moscow, but their fragrance is wonderful." I liked the gentle smile in her calm blue eyes.

"It's good of you to come. Unexpected meetings have a charm of their own. Why didn't you bring Svetlana with you?" I asked.

"Oh! She was planning a long walk in the forest with Shailendra. I was not keen to go with them. Besides, I wanted to ask you for a small favour," she said rather hesitantly.

"It'll be a pleasure if I can do anything for you. Come to think of it, even I wanted to ask you something. Couldn't do that yesterday with so many people around."

I was curious about Svetlana's life. Only Maria would know something about it. "Let's have some coffee in the back lawn," I suggested. "Today the sky is clear and the snow-mountains are visible in all their glory."

After giving saplings to the gardener, as Maria and I walked towards the back lawn, I told her the story of Svetlana's sunbath narrated by Shailendra.

Maria burst out laughing. "Even I would have liked to be in the sun that way. Such bright and sunny days are rare in our country. It's normal for us to enjoy sunbathing in this manner. But, I would have been hesitant to violate the customs of your country. Svetlana has a different attitude. As she once told me, she had to cope with all kinds of difficulties to live life on her own terms, and now she would not give up her hard won freedom at any cost."

Maria had a problem. When she went for a walk in the forest with Shailendra and Svetlana after my visit yesterday, she forgot to take her handbag with her. On her return, she found the bag but the cash in it was missing. It was a big mistake to leave the bag in the room, and she realized there was no possibility of recovering the stolen money. It was no use mentioning it to Svetlana who would have raised an alarm immediately. Maria felt that any such thing would only create problems for Shailendra and vitiate the mood of their holiday.

"I was in a dilemma and couldn't think what to do," Maria said in an embarrassed tone. "Then I remembered you mentioning the previous evening that you were likely to go to Delhi shortly. It occurred to me that perhaps I could request you to help me out. I need only a small amount of money to clear my hotel bill. I will repay you as soon as I reach Delhi."

Her choice of words and graceful manner touched me. I also appreciated her sensitive effort of not disturbing the mood of their vacation for Svetlana's sake. The fact that she felt comfortable to seek my help after just two short meetings, also pleased me.

"A trivial matter!" I said. "You could have just sent me a message instead of bothering to come all this way. But I appreciate your concern for your friend. In your place, Svetlana would have lodged a report with the police without batting an eyelid."

"No, no! It is not like that at all! You shouldn't think so harshly of her. Initially, I too had doubts about her attitude. Difficult circumstances in one's life can break a person, but this girl has lived through unbelievable situations. Sometimes, I think how troubled I feel with minor problems in my simple life. But Svetlana remains so lively in spite of facing innumerable difficulties. I have learnt so much from her."

Maria was quiet for a while. Then, looking at the snow peaks glistening in the bright sunlight, she said, "Didn't you say you also wanted to ask me something?"

"Oh yes!" I replied. "But you've already told me much of what I wanted to know. Yet, I must say that I continue to be surprised seeing you and Svetlana together. Both of you are so different from each other. What is the mystery of this bond between you?"

Maria laughed, "We are not lovers for sure, if that's what is bothering you."

She went on, "I think in our attitude and approach to life we are like the north and south poles of a magnet, and as in physics, the opposite poles attract each other. I have been of a religious temperament right from my childhood. I always felt that the atheistic attitude imposed on our country after the 'October 1917 Revolution' greatly harmed our society. But Svetlana has perhaps not even heard the word 'religion'. As we were walking towards your house last evening, we passed an old church. I wanted to go in and have a look, but Svetlana refused to let me go. 'What kind of foolish, orthodox notions you have,' she said."

"According to Marxists, religion is the opium of the masses," I said. "Before Gorbachev rose to power in your country, this attitude was constantly drummed into the minds of children in every school. I am surprised how you escaped it to continue with your faith in religion."

Maria smiled, "Its perhaps the genes from my previous birth. I think I was born in India in my previous life. Perhaps that is why I come here so often. I've even tried to learn Hindi. Three years ago, a pandit in the holy town of Matan in Kashmir told me that in my last life my name was Maya Devi."

"Maya Devi! The world 'maya' has numerous meanings – miracles, magic, money, wealth, sex, illusory love, etc. I think, many of these apply more to your friend than you."

Maria looked at me in mock anger, and said. "It's not nice of you to find faults of every kind in Svetlana. This is neither good for you nor fair to her. If you try to understand her, you will discover so many positive qualities in her."

"There is no need for you to get upset and defend her. I think she is a very competent and intelligent woman. Perhaps, she has also come to India in search of *moksha (liberation)* to discover the essence of life. It appears to me that while you haven't moved beyond the first stage, she has skipped it and got on to the second and third stages."

She asked, "I don't follow you. What is the essence of life?"

"According to our scriptures," I said, "the ultimate goal of a human being is to attain *moksha,* which is liberation from the cycle of birth and rebirth. One achieves it through a balanced conduct in the three basic areas of life – *dharma, artha, and kama* (ethical conduct, worldly success, and rightful enjoyment of one's senses)."

Maria said, "I cannot understand such high philosophy. I like India because despite all historical ups and downs, and poverty, it is still a deeply religious country. As I see it, the current levels of high illiteracy do not bear any relationship to the inner quality of the life of Indians. They continue to live their simple lives peacefully and conscientiously with the religious beliefs they seem to inherit in their genes."

"I agree with you," I said, "Looking at the way of life in the affluent countries, I feel that modern education and technological developments are forcing them to seek satisfactions of life merely at a physical level, to the neglect of all spiritual urges. And this lifestyle is becoming the benchmark of a superficially good life all over the world. The priority accorded to physical pleasures conditions us to have a casual approach towards emotions, religion and beauty. This is why I appreciate your concern about religion."

The sky was getting cloudy. The rain did not appear imminent, but snow seemed to be falling on the distant high peaks. A strong wind began to blow and the weather turned chilly. I felt that Maria must be shivering in her light yellow shawl. It was half past one.

"Let's go inside. It's time for lunch," I said.

As Maria and I walked to the dining room, she said, "I like what you say, though I don't understand much of it."

I laughed. "To like something is more important than understanding it. Often, I also don't understand many things I hear. Understanding is the activity of our intelligence, which in my view stands at a somewhat lower level than liking something. The great American novelist Hemingway wrote that looking and loving the shape of a tree is a far superior thing than knowing all about its botany," I said.

Maria smiled. "We had an interesting conversation today," she said. "But you wanted to know something about Svetlana and I got you involved in my own talk."

She finished her lunch and kept quiet for a while. Then she said, "Why don't you ask her yourself? If you like, I can ask her to come here tomorrow morning. I will also come of course, to translate the conversation for both of you."

After she left, I wondered what I should ask Svetlana. I had nothing particular in mind. Whatever I saw and heard about her made me curious in a general way. Perhaps it was natural that a glamorous woman so adept at the conscious display of her charms would make any man think about her. But there was something more that excited my curiosity. What kind of difficult situation did she have to cope with at a young age? The struggles she underwent to deal with them? And how did she acquire the capability to live life on her own terms in the midst of all the problems she faced? And it would not be incorrect to say that perhaps unconsciously, I also looked forward to meeting her again.

The next morning, Maria and Svetlana arrived at eleven. Svetlana was dressed in the familiar attire of the previous evening. The same luscious frame; the same confident air; and the same tinge of a playful smile lurking on her lips.

Maria began the conversation. "I have told her that you are impressed by her courage to live so fearlessly.

You wish to know how, unlike me, you acquired such a bold and courageous spirit." She laughed for a moment before continuing. "And, you are also curious about the mystery of our friendship despite our totally dissimilar ways of life."

I liked the way Maria started the meeting. A light-hearted, playful mood of the participants is so conducive to a meaningful conversation.

"That is quite correct," I said "Yesterday, there were so many people here that I didn't really have a chance to talk to you. People surrounded you; everyone was keen to photograph you. I hope the pictures come out well and do justice to the beautiful woman you are. And I was also truly amazed by your ability to pose and bring such varied expressions to your face. Someone, in fact, asked me if you were an actress."

As Maria began to translate my words for Svetlana, I observed the fleeting expressions on Svetlana's face. A gentle smile, a crease on the eyebrows and lips, and then an oblique glance playfully thrown at me. Finally, a thoughtful mood enveloped her face. I had kept looking at her calm face as she responded to Maria. It was as if I could read the thought processes going on in her mind to give shape to her words. I couldn't take my eyes off from the determined look on her face.

Our translator began to convey Svetlana's reply. "Yesterday, after Maria left to meet you, I went out to explore the forest with Shailendra. After a while, we reached a massive rock. Flat at the top, the rock had a sharp drop below its eastern edge. As I looked down from the top, a familiar picture suddenly flashed in front of my eyes. Some treetops and bushes were visible hundreds of feet below me. Shailendra whispered that if someone slipped or jumped down, all sufferings and pains of life would be over in just a few moments. His words echoed a thought that had come to my mind many years ago."

Maria paused, looked at Svetlana for a few moments, and then she continued in a sombre tone, "It was a similar place in the Ural mountains of Siberia, not far from our house. A big flat rock with a sharp and straight drop down into the valley below it. That evening, I stood on the edge of the rock, ready to jump. As I looked down for the last time, a thought similar to what Shailendra said, filled my mind: I could be free of everything in just a few moments."

"Then, miraculously it occurred to me," Maria went on, "that I had perfect freedom to jump any time I wanted; it didn't have to be just at that time. What was the hurry? I could decide it whenever I wanted to. A great sense of freedom suddenly enveloped me."

Gazing at Svetlana's face Maria stopped for a moment, and then she continued with her translation. "At the onset of winter months every year, as a child I was always fascinated, watching the grey flocks of Siberian Cranes flying high in the sky, courageously traversing thousands of miles to faraway India. On that day, standing on the edge of that rock, I realized that I was also always free to do anything I wanted, like the Siberian Cranes."

Maria continued, "As I walked back to my house, all negative thoughts vanished from my mind and I was filled with a strange feeling of liberation. I returned home with a resolute feeling in my heart. And I have not looked back ever since."

I was completely taken aback by Svetlana's story. Maria had kept looking at the flowers in the garden without any expression on her face as she conveyed Svetlana's words to me. I watched Svetlana silently for some time, and then said to Maria, "It was a very disturbing story. May I take the liberty of asking what prompted her to think of jumping off that rock? But I will understand perfectly, if she does not wish to answer my question."

Svetlana responded through Maria, "I told you the story of my free will, and your question is a natural consequence. Maria may have told you that both my parents died in a car accident when I was seventeen. My uncle, who was my father's business partner, took care of me for the next three years. At the end of those years, I was pregnant, and for many weeks before I stood at the edge of the rock that day I was constantly coaxed by him to have an abortion."

Maria continued, "The forty-five minutes I took to walk back home from the rock, changed my life. All my bitter experiences of the last three years and of the weeks after my pregnancy were gone, and I was filled with a strange feeling of strength and purity in my heart. I became light-hearted. Yes, I will give birth to my baby, I said to myself. I realized that love and emotions are the basis of life, and maintaining their purity is the meaning of life. My child will inspire me to keep my feelings clean and pure, and I will do whatever is necessary to preserve that purity. I was prepared to face the world. Yes! I will deal with any situation in the world, I said aloud. And I don't need to announce my resolve to any one in the world; only to keep reassuring my own self always and always."

"Then, I took over my father's business," Maria continued with her friend's story. "Yet, as I worked to create an independent life for myself in a world dominated by men, I realized the impossibility of it without support from men notwithstanding all talk of women's equality. I understood that unlike women, men are constantly looking for sensual pleasures. That was their greatest weakness, and perhaps a woman's greatest opportunity. I also found that most men can be twirled around a smart woman's little finger by a few meaningless, superficial tricks."

We sat quietly for a time after Maria completed her narration. The sky was clear and a bright sun had softened the chill in the air. Bright sunshine would be good for the flowers, I thought. The hour was well past lunch time.

"Let's have lunch," I said.

As we rose from our chairs in the lawn, looking at Svetlana I said to Maria, "If you don't mind, may I ask you one last question?"

As Svetlana nodded in affirmation, I said, "I am intrigued to see the two of you with a totally different mindset as good friends. What is it that attracts and keeps you together? I asked Maria the same question yesterday, but she dismissed it with a flippant reply."

Maria translated my question for Svetlana. Both of them smiled and started talking to each other laughingly. Finally, Maria came up with the reply.

"You are absolutely right," Maria translated, "it was clear to me at our very first meeting that both of us have a totally different lifestyle. Perhaps, it was this which made me curious about the different world of Maria. Then, as we spent some time together, I began to like her world. I liked Maria's simple ways and her easy and unpretentious lifestyle, which was so different from the intrigues of the world of business I had always known and lived in. And with passing years, as my child grew and as I often looked into her innocent and trusting eyes, something in my ways of life started bothering me. My mind began to wonder if that was the kind of life I wanted for my daughter. With such thoughts arising in my mind, I thought of the possibility of sending my daughter to a school in Moscow if I could persuade Maria to agree to be her local guardian."

"But wouldn't that have left you all alone?" I asked.

"I was left alone after the death of my parents. Then, my daughter came into my life, and I know now that I will never be alone again. I know that wherever she lives, her cheerful, smiling face will always remain in my heart."

Maria went on with Svetlana's reply, "I have never gone to a church or to a priest like Maria. I have never read the Bible. But I know that if there is a God, he sends children into the world to teach elders how to lead a good life. And I can see that my daughter is teaching me this without uttering a word."

Svetlana and Maria left for Delhi that night. I did not hear from them for a long time. I received many photographs of Svetlana that my friends had taken during the party held at my house. I sent the photographs to them, but did not get a reply.

After three months, I received a letter from Maria. She wrote that Svetlana loved the photographs. The letter also said that Svetlana had decided to accompany her to Moscow, and had visited many schools. Two months later, Svetlana was back in Moscow with her daughter, after persuading me to keep her under my care. She admitted the girl to a good school in Moscow. Svetlana had decided to shut down her business in Siberia and buy a farm near the Georgian border. She said that the war between Russia and Georgia had reduced the prices of land in that area and it was a good opportunity for her to start a new life.

I never heard from them again. Often, when I go down that scraggy pathway to Shailendra's guesthouse, I see Svetlana. The same black dress; the same high-heeled stilettos; and the same black veil on her face. Then I see Maria going to a school in her jeans and a shirt with a yellow shawl on her shoulders, holding the hand of a little girl. And I keep wondering where all of them are now?

The Return Journey

Reaching halfway to Delhi the air-conditioned bus from Chandigarh had stopped at the newly built picnic resort at Chakravarty Lake. Passengers moved to the restaurant for the half hour break. Some children tried to row a boat in the lake close to the restaurant, oblivious to the heat of the strong sun. Groups of ducks paddling in the lake looked nonchalantly at the zig-zagging boat.

In the air-conditioned coolness of the restaurant, waiters in white uniforms hurriedly took orders from the travellers.

A group consisting of two children, two adults, and two old people sat at a large table near the window. The seven-year-old girl in a red dress and her brother who was two years older were talking to their mother in English with a pronounced American accent.

"I want to catch a duck," the little boy said, making an unsuccessful attempt to rise from his chair to go out of the restaurant. His mother was dressed in a blue and white pant suit. Her bobbed blonde hair already had traces of grey in it. She was a tall thin American woman who looked somewhat older than her husband.

"Preet, we have sandwiches. Just order the coffee, please." She spoke to her husband in English and moved towards the toilet with her daughter.

Harpreet Singh, dressed in brown corduroy trousers and a tee-shirt with "University of Minnesota" printed on it, had lost touch with the five "Ks" of the Sikh religion a long time ago. Despite early indications of obesity of the oncoming middle years, his short trimmed beard looked good on him. Taking advantage of his wife's absence, he started talking to his parents in Panjabi.

"When will you come again?" His mother spoke Panjabi with a heavy colloquial accent. When her daughter-in-law was present, conversation could only be made in English. The children knew just a smattering of Panjabi and Hindi, and the grandmother could not speak English at all. The little boy sitting on a chair near the window ignored his grandmother's hand as it caressed his back. In the speechless meeting of a few days, the only efforts the old grandmother could make to build her relationship with the children were through chocolates and feeble touches of bodily contact.

"Ammi, a possibility may emerge in a few months for me to visit Chandigarh University next year."

The old Sikh father once again carefully read every letter of the words "University of Minnesota" spread across his son's chest. He could not decide whether his son's reply was truthful or merely a sop to stem the tears welling up in his mother's eyes. He looked expectantly towards his son who was busy placing his order for pakoras and coffee, savouring every word of the Panjabi dialect he chose to speak in. The Haryanvi waiter made a point of answering him in Hindi though he could clearly speak in Panjabi as well. He was in a hurry to take the order and move to another table. Perhaps he understood that Harpreet Singh needed to hear the sound of Panjabi more than the coffee. But the charges for the extra time spent in speaking Panjabi could not be added to the bill.

A little girl at the adjoining table was trying to use a knife and fork to eat a cutlet.

"Child, why don't you use your hands?" Harpreet said to her.

The reply came from the child's mother. "Children have become very fashionable these days."

"I agree with you," Harpreet Singh said." "My daughter likes to eat even a mango with a spoon."

"Do you live abroad?" the woman asked.

Harpreet was somewhat dismayed by the question. Attempting to keep the conversation out of his mother's hearing range, he replied in English, "Yes. In fact we are taking the flight to New York tonight. But I always return to India every three-four years."

The boat zig-zagging in the lake had crashed against the concrete banks. Two boys in the boat struggled to control the oars.

A big white cloud had risen in the sky. Its tall shadow spread from the boat to the window-sill in the restaurant. The little boy sitting near the window felt the tension of his father's over enthusiastic conversation and the unnaturally silent response of the grandparents. He stuffed his mouth with sandwiches.

When the waiter brought pakoras and coffee, his grandmother filled the child's plate with pakoras and spread tomato ketchup on them. She had apparently run out of her stock of chocolates. Notwithstanding her difficulties with the language, her principal way of demonstrating affection had always been an insistence on over-feeding. "Mummy, all this fried stuff will upset his stomach." The daughter-in-law returning from the toilet spoke up from a distance.

"Preet, please explain to your mother. We will have problems on the flight."

Harpreet Singh leaned towards his mother, "Ammi, it is time for him to get back to American food."

The little boy tried once more to get up and walk out, in an effort to get away from the scene. "I want to catch a duck," he said.

Harpeet's wife looked at the time in her wrist watch. "Preet, please take him to the toilet. We still have time."

The little girl in her grandmother's lap tried to wriggle out. The old grandmother's eyes were fixed on Harpreet. He had come after four years and the days had flown by so quickly. In the emptiness of old age, four years appeared longer than a whole lifetime.

"Mummy, your coffee." The daughter-in-law filled the cup but the old lady was lost in dreams of the remote past. Memories of the past years filled her mind.

"This place is well designed. It seems to be newly constructed." The daughter-in-law examined the wood-panelled walls of the restaurant.

The little boy, his father, and the grandfather were the last passengers of the air-conditioned bus to use the toilet. Outside the air-conditioned spaces, the weather was hot and sultry. Compelled to sit on the toilet seat, the little boy listened to the conversation between his father and grandfather.

"Tissue paper is used in America even to wipe one's nose," Harpreet explained to his old father.

"Why? Is there a shortage of water?" asked the old man. "How can you be clean without water?"

The little boy pulled out long lengths of toilet paper from the paper roll hanging near the toilet seat.

"Don't waste that paper!" Harpreet yelled at the boy. Then he continued with his father. "I always use water. The children are accustomed to using both water and paper."

By the time they came back to the restaurant, most of the passengers had finished their meal and were returning to the bus. The little girl had escaped from her grandmother's lap and stood with her nose hard pressed against the window pane. She watched the ducks weaving their way around the boats in the lake. The waiter picked up the bill tray and gave a big salaam to the wife. He had received a hefty tip. The grandmother was searching something undefined in the misty whiteness of the big cloud in the sky beyond the window.

The wife looked at her wrist watch as she climbed into the air-conditioned bus. There were only five hours left now for the return flight.

An Unfinished Story

"Bijli Mahadev? What a strange name!"

"Take the short-cut, sir. The cottage is just three and a half miles from the bridge," the agent said.

It was the middle of March. In the clear morning sky we could see the mountain peaks glistening with fresh snow that had fallen at night. A cold wind blew from the mountain slopes above Kulu but the open ground in front of the tourist bungalow was warmed by the sharp sun.

In those days property sales had not yet become big business and there was only one estate agent in Kulu. I was lucky to have caught him that morning. After months of investigations, I was convinced that land should still be cheap on the mountain slopes above the valley.

"A jeepable road would be ready towards the end of next year. It is a part of the new project to connect Bijli Mahadev with Naggar. Work has already begun."

There was snow on top of Bijli Mahadev. Across the river, on the bank opposite Kulu township, the mountain rose to a great height. Halfway up the mountain slope a seven-acre orchard was up for sale.

"An apple tree needs six years to bear fruit", the agent explained. "The first crop was harvested last year. The trees are of the best quality. You should see them in early August when they are heavy with fruit."

The name of the mountain intrigued me. Bijli Mahadev! What a peculiar name. But at the quoted price the orchard was a bargain. "Why should anyone sell at such a low price? There must be a catch somewhere," I thought. The orchard was only three and a half miles away, I could easily be back before sundown.

"Will the owner be at the orchard now?" I enquired.

"I have sent him word to expect you, but he is unpredictable. I hear that he spends a lot of time these days riding around in the forest near the mountain top," the agent replied. "About a month ago he had come down to the bazaar to see off his wife on the bus to Chandigardh. A month after that, I received a letter mentioning his intention to sell the orchard. His wife has not been back since. She is a very beautiful woman."

"Why did he decide to sell the orchard?"

"I don't know, sir. I am surprised myself. He worked so hard to plant the trees, and spent several months every year at the orchard for the last eight years. The cottage was remodelled two years ago when he was thinking of moving permanently to the orchard."

"Something must have happened. There has to be a reason." I persisted in my question.

"It is hard to say, sir. It may have been a quarrel with his wife. Last year when she was here, they used to wander all over the valley. They crossed the Rohtang Pass when it was covered under five feet of snow. This year we have hardly seen her anywhere in the valley. She is a beautiful woman."

The sun shone brightly on the eastern slopes of Bijli Mahadev. It was already half past ten. The orchard was at an elevation of about six thousand feet. There would never be much snow there, I thought. The sunlight on the eastern slopes was weaker than on the western slopes. "The site has been chosen well," I thought. "If it was higher, there would be too much snow. This elevation is just perfect."

Across the river, a narrow footpath wound its way up the hill. The lower slopes had terraced fields with pools of water in them. Above the fields there were barren stretches of rock interspersed with scraggy bushes. The mountain top was covered by a cedar forest.

"Is it easy to find porters to carry baggage up to the orchard?? I enquired.

"No problem, sir. When work on the road picks up, there may be a shortage of porters. But by then the road would almost be ready." The orchard was a bargain notwithstanding the high commission of the agent.

"It is an excellent proposition, sir," the agent went on. "The cottage has been enlarged into a beautiful bungalow with all around glazing. It is so cheerful. You will be pleased to see it." The agent was not prepared to accompany me to the orchard. It was not even necessary.

When I reached the orchard it was past midday. The chowkidar said that Mr. Paul had waited for me all morning. He had just gone for a ride in the forest and was expected back in an hour's time.

The house surrounded by the orchard was indeed beautiful. Every room carried an indelible mark of its owner's taste. Sunlight streamed through the glass-roofed verandah. The living room was pleasantly warm. It overlooked the valley and had an excellent view of the snow ranges. The chowkidar knew that I had come to negotiate the sale of the orchard.

"Why is Paul Saheb selling the orchard?" I asked him.

The chowkidar was quiet for an instant. Then he said, "Last year Saheb told me that he would buy the adjoining land and plant more trees. We had a very good crop last year. I have no idea why he has decided to sell it now. It is God's will."

The orchard was neatly laid out, the road was under construction, and Kulu township was close by. I could not have hoped for a better place. When Paul returned late in the afternoon, we took less than an hour to complete the details of the sale.

The sun was low over the hill in front of us. The evening was setting in.

"Will you have a glass of *chaang*?" he asked.

"*Chaang*?"

"Have you ever tasted it? You must try it." He poured me a large tumbler containing a warm liquid that looked like whey. "The Tibetans can drink large quantities of it during the course of an evening. Some Tibetan families worked on the orchard at harvest time last year. I learnt about this brew from them."

I liked *chaang*. It was warm and only mildly intoxicating. We sat in the glass-roofed verandah room. The last rays of sun filtered through the window and fell on Paul's face.

He must be about thirty-five, I thought.

"It is warm in here," I said.

"Yes, the glass lets the sun in, and it retains the heat, keeping the room warm. The glass roofing has been a good job."

"Did your wife design the cottage?" I could not restrain my curiosity.

Paul stared out of the window for a long time.

"I am not married," he said.

"I am sorry,"

"It does not matter. She was a friend. The cottage was designed by her."

The sky was turning cloudy. Night would fall earlier than I expected. I had told the chowkidar at the tourist bungalow that I would be back before it got dark.

"I am leaving Kulu by the seven-thirty bus tomorrow morning." I got up to leave.

But Paul insisted that I spend the night at the cottage. The *chaang* was good, and Paul said that there were two kettlefuls more in the kitchen. It would not take me long to walk down in the morning, I thought. The soft warmth of the room was also pleasing. Outside the room it must already be freezingly cold.

"Why didn't you get married?" I asked.

Paul looked out of the window. The sun was setting behind the hill. His face was lit up with the last rays of the sun.

"I do not really know. Life comes to us in strange ways. Marriage seems to have drifted away from me."

"Everyone finds a wife. It is the normal order of life."

"I don't know. One is tempted to follow time-tested conventions. And then so many other ideas float into the mind. I have often wondered about the kind of happiness which results from ordering one's life firmly."

I took a long sip of *chaang*. The sun had set. Darkness was enveloping the valley. Soon it would be night.

"Isn't it true," I said, "that one discards one set of conventions only to be caught by another set? We can rationalize anything we set our mind on. I think when we are confused, there is a need to reassure oneself with all kinds of new ideas."

Paul laughed. "You've got high rather quickly. The speciality of *chaang* is that one begins to philosophize after two glasses. Poetry flows when you get to the fourth one."

"I don't understand philosophy." I replied, "But I do believe that if one speaks with an open heart, there will be no misunderstandings. Without faith and trust people build walls around themselves. How can there be any happiness with such individualism?"

"Do you really believe people deliberately build walls around them and open-heartedness can pull them down?"

The chowkidar brought us another kettle of *chaang*.

"Let's finish this. Then we can have dinner," Paul said. In the increasing darkness, we could see the lights of Kulu in the valley below us. We sat for some time drinking *chaang* in a companionable silence.

After filling his glass from the kettle, Paul said, "Don't you believe that human beings have rhythms of their own whose vibrations are unknown and uncontrollable by them. I think only a small part of our lives is governed by reason, by what should happen logically. But, isn't most of life dominated by instinctual responses? Aren't we the prisoners of our instincts most of the time? Isn't our unconscious mind the principal driving force of life?"

As we left the verandah room, we felt the cold wind that was sweeping the mountain side. The moon had not yet risen. The wind had blown away the clouds and the sky was starlit. In the stillness of the night I could hear the sound of a distant waterfall.

Paul stood by the door staring into the dark valley. "Years ago my father was posted in Kulu as a senior government official. I spent my childhood in the forests and snows. I inhaled the intoxicating freshness of the pine-perfumed mountain breezes. It is this air, sun and mountains that make a man open-hearted and trusting. I have known the magic of this world. And I also know that there are spaces in our heart that we cannot penetrate ourselves. Perhaps it is the uncertainty of reaching these spaces that keeps our spirit alive to the mystery of life. Love and faith cannot answer everything because life has no ultimate conclusions. Perhaps they can only enable us to respect others and believe that an individual has no option but to pursue his own mysterious path to deal with his life."

The chowkidar cleared the plates. It was past eleven o'clock. We walked back to the main house. My bed was made in one of the inner rooms with a lamp by the bedside. The mountain slopes were all sliver in the moonlight.

"As I had mentioned, one begins to philosophize after a kettle of *chaang*. You have to leave early in the morning. You must go to bed before you start on poetry."

"Why are you selling the orchard?" I asked.

Paul stopped at the door to the inner room. "Sandhya finally went away last month. Over the years, this earth and air had absorbed so much of her that it is not possible for me to stay here any longer."

He continued, "You may think that I am not talking sensibly. But I think when we begin to think too much, it becomes difficult to arrive at clear conclusions; we are beset by doubts. Logical analysis builds its own walls. We want things to flow like the leaves falling in the waters of a river. But somehow everything goes haywire.

After putting out the lamp, I lay awake in my bed for a long time wondering at the bargain I had made in purchasing the orchard, and about Sandhya who was not there but whose invisible presence was everywhere. It was a beautiful orchard. Paul had mentioned that the trees would blossom next month, and the snow above the pine forest would melt soon after that. Paul went off to sleep in his room and he was still asleep when I left the next morning. I did not meet him again.

Two months later when I returned to Kulu to check on the crop of my newly acquired orchard, there was a short note from Paul waiting for me at the agent's office.

"There are a few letters in the top drawer of the writing table in the verandah room. Some that Sandhya wrote to me, and some which I sent her. She could not destroy them and left them with me. You may remember, I had mentioned that in the flow of life we wish to discard many things. We want to and yet we cannot. I could not destroy these letters though I tried to many times. I am leaving them behind. You may destroy them or do whatever you wish to do with them, but do not send them back to me."

I could not destroy the letters. I had thought that in the long winter evenings I would sit in the verandah room overlooking the snow mountains and reconstruct the story of Paul and Sandhya. But I could not do that. The letters seemed to have an unfinished life of their own, and it was not possible for me to complete their story. It is perhaps only possible to reproduce them.

24th July

I returned to this house in the hills—so dear to me—after many days to find two letters from you. The maid had kept them carefully. She did not show them to anyone or even get them redirected to me. She recognizes your handwriting.

I am in the verandah room, looking at the clouds outside the window. Clouds have such beautiful shapes. In these hills, fog and mist rise from all sides to cover everything in their white mystery, even the human mind. I did not even realize that the chowkidar had come into the room ten minutes ago.

Bhaiya had come up a few days ago. He talked about you, and just kept talking. He said such flattering things about you and asked me if I had met you. After he left,

I walked out into the garden. Felt like writing you a long … long letter. You always complain that I take a long time to reply to your letters. Believe me, when I receive a letter from you, I want to pick up a pen and just keep writing till the paper takes in every shade of my feelings. And then, hesitations fill my mind. I feel that perhaps later, when balance and reason return, the lines written in these moments of emotional upsurge may leave both of us embarrassed. I get lost in my thoughts. Then I see that above the trees, the sky is full of clouds. Why do so few people look at the sky?

Yesterday, I was thinking of our picnic at the Qutub. I would love to go there again. What a beautiful day it was. Avadesh was also talking about it. He is so warm-hearted, but doesn't seem to understand our situation.

When will the trees in the orchard blossom? I have seen apple blossom once—a beautiful shade of purple. I wonder if it will snow in the garden? I have never seen falling snow.

25th January

I should not write you long letters as I have done for so many years. A friend once told me that long letters only lead to misunderstandings. What is the use of these letters then? Mere words. Anyway, you live in a dream world of your own. And I just keep writing. It is a month since my transfer to this place—a small town. Just a few families who only mix with each other. There is little outside contact. It is strange to observe men and women in this close inner circle. Women, especially the newly married ones, appear to be poles apart from their men in their vision of life. Men fall into conventional patterns so easily. Perhaps the changing values of our society give shape to a life in which right from adolescence we are attracted only by the physical glitter of things—by dreams of material success—leaving a vacuum in the emotional layers for a whole lifetime.

I do not really know why I am writing this. I wonder what you will say when you read these lines. Often I feel that my letters are so selfishly written, filling sheets of paper with just anything that floats into my mind. But then, what else can I write?

Avadesh wrote, I do not know if it is right for me to say so but I think that under the pretext of compassion, of not hurting his sentiments, you keep his illusions alive. Perhaps you do not see the impropriety of this. Perhaps some part of your inner system needs to keep things as they are. But enough of this, especially since I cannot even pretend to be a neutral party. My only recourse is to pen and paper. Time and place—physical circumstance—shape so much of our lives.

There is a tree in the garden in front of my room. Its dark leaves acquire a velvety softness in the fading light of the evening. There is a serene beauty in this deep green which I enjoy looking at in the silence of evening. When the colour of the leaves gets lighter, it loses this serene beauty, acquiring a flippant playful mood. I wonder if this tree will grow in the garden of the Kulu house. The orchard of the house should have its first crop next year. The cottage needs to be remodelled. When will I see you? Even when we meet, you are always trying to disappear somewhere. Believe me, nobody can put a *nazar* on you.

What plans are you making for the future? Life can only be shaped with well thought out choices and actions. Will you dispute even this?

10th May

The train must have left by now. I phoned at eight. You had left for the station. Our phone was not working and the neighbours with a phone did not return home till eight. I wanted to take a taxi and come to the station but there was no time left.

All day long I had repeated to myself everything I wanted to say to you. How easy it had seemed, and I smiled to think how happy you would have been to hear them.

I feel so helpless. Papa did not let me leave the house the whole day. You must be in the train. I could not even give you an answer.

11th May

Your brief note from the station. It is good that you have no misconceptions left. Misconceptions make us lose so much. I posted a letter to you yesterday. You are right, as always. I agree that life can only make sense if firm decisions are taken.

25th October

Your letter arrived only yesterday. You wrote after a long silence. New places and experiences must occupy you. It will be a new way of life. Your short letter reverberates with your new mood, which is good. A little flippancy attaches itself to success but a thinking person soon rises above it. When the horizon suddenly widens, the mind fills with innumerable possibilities and expectations. And then, after a while, one realizes that an enlargement only of the physical situations does not mean much in the overall movement of life.

But understanding comes only with one's own experience. There is no other way to it. Others can help to analyse and enlarge an experience, but they can never make you see anything which you have not experienced yourself. I can only say that your present mood is preferable to that of a few months ago.

Over the years, I have known the feeling of despair and diffidence when the whole world appears to crumble and collapse. And I know that one cannot avoid such moments for they are an integral part of the human situation. When I think dispassionately, every state of mind has its own rewards. Sometimes despondency, exhaustion and defeat lead to the regeneration of a finer sensitivity. Against this, the joyous upsurge of success tends to ride rough-shod over many subtle feelings. But then, it has its own beauty of affirmative action by the creative forces of life.

I had first known you in this joyous mood. There was self-confident pride and the innocent spirit of youth, it seemed that the world was at your feet. I had then thought that as life goes on, its struggles would make dents in this self-confidence. Pride would then fight back to reassert confidence, and the cycle would continue. That is how life seems to treat us all. What am I writing about? Does it make any sense to you? But it is such a pleasant feeling writing to you. So many thoughts and feelings, hiding in secret nooks and corners of my mind, censored by reason, rise to the surface. But then, there is the danger of drifting aimlessly. This is what happens to me most of the time.

Often, the world appears strange to me. For most human beings, the roulette of life stops at a fixed point, very early, and they settle down to a dull routine. It becomes a slow cart, moving along a beaten track, without any real spirit or faith in one's own inclinations.

Often I wish that my life would also flow at a peaceful pace, no matter how simplistic, naïve, or fragile that be. And then you, the thought of whom brings so much joy and torment to me. The mind has an infinite capacity for make-belief, for fooling oneself. We make constant efforts to understand ourselves and to establish harmonious relationships, but where does anyone reach finally? All our efforts seem predestined to failure.

It is many months since I heard from you. I thought our friendship had come to an end. But it appears that both of us are caught by the pull of an undefinable tension sustained through these letters, and this paper relationship continues. What subterfuges one invents! How mischievous was your reference to a platonic friendship? I remember the transparent waters of the lake where we had gone for a picnic last year. Why can't our lives be like that? You were wearing a red bathing costume. I see the image so vividly, and then it shifts. It brings an excitement of a different order, with its link to the past. The costume falls, the top and then altogether and the figure steps into the clear waters of the lake—fresh, cheerful, as if heralding a new beginning. What is a platonic relationship? A friendship is a friendship, and if it is honest, strong, and enduring, there is no need for explanations and qualifications. What is the use of these hollow pretensions to a pseudo-morality?

You are getting entangled in a web of self-created contradictions. You have known Avadhesh for years. Willingly you chose to believe what you wanted to believe. That poor man has hung on for nothing.

What is to be gained by analysis? It is impossible to reach any conclusions in an emotional situation through analysis because our mind piles up arguments justifying contradictory viewpoints. The main thing is life itself, which has sunshine, air, earth, the warmth of a human body. Where the fragrance of flowers, trees and living creatures overwhelm the spirit. All other things are only the means to reach this end. We try to understand it and find harmony with it.

I have written so much and am caught in those illusory-wishful-flights of imagination against which I have been arguing.

There are two cats here who often drink the glass of milk which the servant keeps on my bedside table. I battled with the cats for many days, but we are friends now. Next time I will write only about the cats.

15th July

After a long time I came to this viewing point at the far end of the Camel's Back Road. It is the rainy season again. I thought I would sit here and write to you. The clouds are drifting in the valley. Stray gusts of wind bring a fine spray to this bench. The mountains are so fresh. The valley below the drifting clouds has been washed anew by the rain. If life could also be washed clean to start afresh. I drift with the clouds. Images of bygone years float into my mind.

You were here last month. What a strange morning it was. There was stillness in the air. A few clouds lay unmoving in the sky. I felt that everything should just stay the way it was. We should keep walking. The *pallu* of my sari should keep flying the same way to touch your hands. The Camel's Back Road should keep vanishing behind its innumerable bends. There were so many things I wanted to tell you. But the silent, peaceful mood of the morning enveloped me. We walked past the viewing point. The pine trees near the cemetery looked so beautiful.

Sitting on the bench, I remember you saying that I live in a world of my dreams. The rain stirs my memories. The clouds, the sound of falling rain, the dancing leaves of the rhododendron trees stir memories of time so precious to me. A lake fills up, immersing my mind in it.

Another year has gone by. Avadhesh has already sent me a gift for my birthday, lest it be delayed by the post office. He is such a gentle tender person. Mami was talking to me last week. She was worried that I am so emotional. She wants me to keep my feet firmly on the ground. "You are not getting any younger. You will be sorry later on. Freedom, independence, your job, these are amusements of a limited period. He is such an understanding man. You must think of what is good for you. Not loving him is no reason. You will always have your way with him, he is so devoted, so dominated by you."

My mind filled with sadness. What kind of calculation was this? Does experience of life and maturity only mean physical convenience, oblivious to every other sentiment? I do not want to dominate or be dominated by anyone. Is it so impractical to want to be just a friend, a woman, and not a traditional wife?

I have learnt so much from you. I am not making you responsible for my mistakes. For so many things that I understand now, I can only convey my gratitude to you. Without your friendship and emotional support many areas of sensibility, which have made my life so much richer, would perhaps not have found depth and maturity. Believe me, it is so enriching to be able to trust someone—to feel easy and free to openly share everything in one's heart with someone. Without such nourishment, so many corners of the human heart dry up for all times.

What can I really say about Avadesh? I do not know why, how, I lost my direction, made my mistakes. I could never learn to cope with the practicalities of life even as I know that finally it is only them which keep one from getting defeated. But Avadesh was so wise and knew everything from the beginning and chose not to know deliberately. You once told me that charity was a shallow sentiment and anything done out of a sense of charity was superficial. I agreed. To receive charity, or to extend it to others, is a weakness. What does is resolve finally?

Do you like this handmade paper? I brought it last year and left it locked in my cupboard here. This is the last sheet. There is also not much more for me to write. The rain has stopped. The clouds have cleared and the last rays of the evening sun are on the balcony. The shadows of the trees are lengthening. How sharp are the outlines of these shadows in the afternoons. And now they are gentle, dissolving into the softness of the evening. Nature is so harmonious and yet so impersonal so indifferent to us. When I was a child, I thought that the world revolves around me. One learns slowly that life or the world does not revolve around anyone. It only revolves around itself with a dispassionate, nonchalant disregard for human fate.

Your cottage must be ready now. I am glad that you liked my designs. I will come to see it next month. At last, I have the freedom to travel without any social or economic barriers. Are you still determined to stay there permanently?

Human life is a strange drama—a play of puppets. Sometimes we are spectators, and at other times puppets. And sometimes we are the puppeteers pulling the strings ourselves. Why are we then surprised at human beings getting lost in doubts and uncertainties? As I grow older, I begin to understand that walls between people are perhaps inherent in the human condition…..

15th February

Today, I decided that I would stay permanently at the orchard.

A storm had raged all night and it snowed early in the morning. I have been pacing up and down in the verandah room. Now the sky is clear. The sun should soon be out. I have established new ties of intimacy with this house, with these trees and mountains. They are now my companions. A bend in the road of life which leaves all the earlier paths behind. I have no choice but to make a new beginning.

The morning has a freshness and the air is crisp. My mind is free of the weight of past years. The atmosphere could not be better to herald a fresh start. I am writing to ask you to be my wife. I would have liked to ask this question looking at you in the freshness of this breeze instead of struggling with these words inscribed on paper in cold ink. I would have liked to hold you close, touch your lips and feel the warmth of your body. But you are not here in spite of my hoping that you would be.

The institution of marriage has never inspired me. It ends up all too often by corroding the personalities of both husband and wife. The security of marriage eliminates the necessity of constant efforts to grow mentally and to keep oneself presentable in body and spirit. Social pressure keeps the institution going even as people become indifferent, frequently unfaithful, bored and irritated with each other.

I have always believed that freedom in its widest sense is the path most conducive to achievement of the highest potential of human personality. Only in freedom can there be that grace and dignity without which life has no meaning. Human life is like a tree which grows, flowers, and bears fruit. The leaves fall every autumn, and then sprout afresh in the spring. And one day the tree falls. What else can we say about life?

One hears so much about marriage being a serious step. It presents a picture of responsibilities and bindings. I am suspicious of serious things. So often seriousness is only a façade to hide one's weaknesses, incapabilities and fears. Openness of human spirit has always been the base on which everything beautiful and serious is built. Calling for responsibilities and bindings reflects only the fears of a stagnant mind. How can love and faith find a place in the midst of them?

But then, marriage is perhaps a commitment that enables a relationship to develop, protected against the pressures of everyday life. It is a framework in which a harmonious intermingling of two beings takes place. This institution cannot achieve anything more. But if we analyse our own lives over the past years we can understand that this in itself is a lot. There is a wildness in the human spirit which longs to fly out. The bond of affection brings a balance and gives it an inward direction.

I await your reply.

19th February

Your letter to me. The envelope had my name on it. As I opened and read it, I looked in vain for an opening to read beyond the lines written in your hand so familiar and dear to me. I am sending it back to remain with you. Keep it safely. One day I may have so many things to ask you.

Images arise in my mind. A red sari with the gold of its *pallu* shimmering against the leaping flames. The fragrance of *samagri* smoke above the golden yellow of the flames. The crackling sound of fire occasionally breaking the recitation of the old man sitting cross-legged across the fire with several lines of white paste on this forehead. In the glow of flickering flames there are smiling faces of elegantly dressed men and women sitting around the fire. No one will photograph the images for me. As always, they will remain only in my mind.

The years will roll by. Sometimes the heart grows heavy like the dark clouds of an overcast sky, sometimes it is clear, and sometimes there is a downpour. You understand so much and write so well. Often, I am not able to write anything clearly. Like the fog and mist of the mountains, vague and dreamy images fill my mind. I see the verdant hills through the moving clouds, and then they get lost. But even a fleeting glimpse of the greenery behind the misty screen of drifting clouds is so dear to me.

I must stop. What else remains to be written?

The road to the orchard has been completed. I go up several times a year. The crops have been good. I wonder if there will be any more letters. And if she will ever come to the cottage again. I feel that some day both of them will return. It is this feeling which draws me to the orchard so often.

★★★

The Flood

Major Sadashiv, Commanding Officer 670 Construction Company, had a physiognomy which was a fair counterpart of the quality of his mind. He was of medium height with an ordinary impassive face and an unruffled steady gait which reflected his contented acceptance, after eighteen years in the army, of no possibility of promotion in the remaining ten years of service before retirement. It was not that he had not eagerly awaited the promotion list till his final year in the promotion zone. But when his name did not appear in the list, his characteristically state of tranquillity did not get unduly disturbed. With his limited span of imagination, he could not recollect any major mistakes made in his career, but he could also not think of any significant achievements either. He knew that only fourteen per cent of the officers could figure in the promotion list, and as he did not have a godfather among the senior officers, he considered it only proper to dismiss this issue.

With his unimaginative style, it had not been possible for him to do anything extraordinary to be noticed by his superiors. At the same time, he had seldom interfered with the daily work of his subordinates and in the course of his relaxed undemanding career he had always received cooperation from them. Free from tensions of work, and of undue anxiety for promotion, his steady and secure career in the army had become an easy way of life. But if he was ever asked why a High School teacher's son had chosen to join the army, he could not have given a satisfactory answer. The event must have been an extraordinary one for his small town, but such distant recollections were beyond his faculties.

In the course of successive years in service, he regularly sent letters to his parents giving a factual account of his life in the army. "It is very cold here during the parade at seven in the morning", "It is the Brigade commander's inspection tomorrow". "The rainfall here is a hundred and ten inches per year, everyone has been issued gumboots". It was a world very different from what he had seen at home since his childhood, and he communicated the events to his father and mother without much comment. At the age of twenty-five, when he was promoted to the rank of a captain, he married—obedient to the wishes and choice of his parents. In the passing years, his wife gave birth to a boy and two girls.

All these events took place many years before the afternoon when in his tented office below the dak bungalow at Menshithang, he asked the chowkidar, "You mean to say that it has been raining continuously for the past three days?"

The tall well-built Khampa chowkidar had travelled twenty miles downhill to the headquarters for his pay from his windswept wooden hut near the snow-fed green lakes at a height of fourteen thousand feet. His weather-beaten face was smeared with yak butter. Constant exposure to the sharp sun and piercing winds of the mountains had toughened his skin till it was like the rawhide of the jacket he wore.

"But the water level in the lakes is lower than what it was last year, though it has been snowing heavily in the mountains," the chowkidar replied.

"Seventh September," Major Sadashiv said to himself as he looked at the calendar on his table. "It was twenty-eighth August last year, and third September the year before".

In the course of his camp inspection the previous week, he had paid special attention to ensure that all tents were pitched above the level of floods in the previous years. This recollection brought a measure of reassurance to Major Sadashiv.

"It is just a matter of a few days," he thought, "then there will be no chance of the flood this year."

The 670 Construction Company was deployed in North Sikkim to build a road between Lachen and

Chungthang. Lachen is the last village on the mule track leading to the eighteen thousand feet high Donkila pass on the Tibet border. Lachen river originates near the pass and descends into a deep gorge half a mile below Lachen village. The road, climbing up from Menshithang valley, rises through the sheer face of the gorge which reverberates with the roar of the stream. It was blasted across the steep slopes of the gorge, and two miles below Lachen it crosses the river on a Bailey Bridge. The river bed is far below the bridge and only the sound of water cascading against the rocks indicates of the force of the stream. Beyond the bridge, the road turns sharply into a pine forest below Lachen which is full of orchards. There are tall cedar trees above Lachen village and finally, near the end of the tree line, there are Bhoj trees.

A few months after missing his name in the promotion list last year, when Major Sadashiv received an offer of a three-year assignment with the para-military Border Roads Organization which carried, besides additional allowances and field facilities, provision of a house for the separated family, he did not hesitate to accept it.

Besides one Subedar, two Havildars, and a Lance Naik, the 670 Construction Company did not employ any army personnel even though the organization was modelled on the army pattern. Initially Major Sadashiv found the conditions awkward, but with time he had no difficulty in adjusting to them. An ability to adjust to varying circumstances was a direct benefit of his easy attitude.

"Report to Two I.C. Sahib", he instructed the chowkidar.

After the tall Khampa chowkidar moved away, Major Sadashiv looked at the line of tents in the Tibetan labour camp on a slope beyond the helipad. Last year, the flood waters had risen to a level just three feet short of the helipad. Against the hill, the tents and the multi-coloured prayer flags of the labour camp looked like flowers of early spring that blossom soon after the snows melt.

Assistant Executive Engineer Sharma, the Two I.C. Sahib, was second in command of the 670 Construction Company. He had completed two and a half years of his four-year contract with the Border Roads Organization. After knocking about a succession of jobs for a year on completion of his engineering degree, he arrived at the conclusion that what you know was less important than whom you knew. He was born into an ordinary family in a village of Rohtak district. He neither knew anyone of importance nor was it possible for him to find any such person. He realized that the only way for him was the difficult route of hard work. In the course of four years to be spent in the jungles with the Border Roads, he hoped to save enough money to get a higher degree from a well-known foreign university.

"Is the ice cracking? Any avalanches?" Sharma asked the chowkidar. Sharma was not stationed in this area last year, but he had heard that more than a hundred people had died in the flood, and dead bodies were found as far as a hundred miles downstream in the Teesta river.

"The level in the lakes is not as high as it was last year," the chowkiar repeated. "But, it has been snowing in the mountains for the last three days."

"Is any snow sliding into the lake?" Sharma enquired again.

"No, Saheb."

It was believed that the sliding of a heavy avalanche into the lakes had caused the flood last year.

"September is a bad month," he thought. "Intermittent rain and sunshine crack the top soil."

At eight o'clock in the evening, Subedar Banta Singh reported to Sharma at the Officer's Mess that the river level had receded by about a foot. The rain had stopped and there was no wind. In the clear night, snow glistened on the mountains above the Lachen village. The roar of the swollen river reverberated through the valley.

"After the flood last year, a team of officers from the Geological Survey was sent here for a holiday at the government's expense. They came here only to create problems for us," Sharma said. "This year, if there is no flood, a team from the Anthropological Survey is expected to study the lifestyle of our Tibeten labourers. Doctor, you will have to look after that team."

Major Sadashiv sat on a chair near the fire. He looked at Sharma once and went back to his magazine. Twenty-five-year-old Dr. Pillai was seated at the other end of the room reading the week-old newspapers brought by the courier that evening.

"Mr. Sharma, as per rules, the Medical Officer cannot be given any administrative responsibility," the doctor replied.

Dr. Pillai was born into a poor family. He had completed his education by securing a government loan which he now repayed in monthly instalments. Poverty and an awareness of his humble background had impelled him to work hard, which won him a gold medal in his final examinations. He was obsessed by an awareness of his impoverished condition. A sense of inferiority and then a feeling of intellectual superiority over his fellow students had led his introverted personality to withdraw into a shell. He concentrated on his studies and shunned experiences of life beyond the classroom. After completing his studies, as he moved into the open world, its unfamiliar ways caught him unawares. He found employment in this para-military organization but could not come to terms with this way of life.

"Doctor, instead of wasting your time on studying military law, if you concentrated on medical proficiency, you might earn rapid promotions," Sharma baited him.

The doctor looked at Sharma with fire in his eyes. Major Sadashiv chose to remain absorbed in his magazine enjoying the warmth of the fire leaping in the grate. He did not want to permit any trivialities to disturb the relief he felt at the news of the receding water level in the river. Outside the window, the clouds had cleared and the sky was strewn with stars. It was not that Major Sadashiv had no complaints against the doctor. It was only because of his phlegmatic nature that he had refrained from taking any strong action against him. Only recently the doctor had refused to give him an injection in his room, stating that according to rules injection could only be given in the medical inspection room.

"Any other OC would have punished the doctor outright, or posted him to a camp at fourteen thousand feet where he could coolly contemplate the rules," Sharma said.

Why Major Sadashiv did not take any such action, can only be a matter of speculation. Perhaps he sympathized with the anguish that the doctor went through in coping with his job in this wild isolated place. It could also be that he chose not to take stern action to avoid adding to his headaches. Be that as it may, Major Sadashiv disregarded the conversation between Assistant Executive Engineer Sharma and Dr. Pillai in the Officers' Mess that evening, though it did not conform to the code of conduct expected from the officers in the Army. He did not want anything to disturb his sense of release from the tension which mounted with the possibility of the flood. But it would also not be correct to say that he did not silently enjoy Sharma's riling the doctor.

"I hear, the labour mate's wife has complained to the colonel that Dr. Pillai examines Tibetan female patients after closing the doors of the medical inspection room, as per rules of course!" Sharma said. "A good looking lady doctor is likely to be posted here shortly."

Beyond the football field, sounds of festivity could be heard emitting from the Tibetan labour camp. Perhaps they had learnt of the receding water level in the river. The tents of the camp were pitched on a high ground. Below them, groups of people had collected around a log fire burning on the flat space used for playing football.

Dr. Pillai folded the last of the newspapers and said, "you will have fun then."

Sharma was waiting for Pillai's reply. "My friends, you have all the fun now. Why shouldn't we have some?"

Dr. Pillai walked out of the Officers' Mess in an effort to control his temper. Outside the Mess, a gravelled road led to the football field. Rain-soaked gravel reflected the moonlight brilliantly. Dark shadows of pine trees criss-crossed the road. The music from the football field rose steadily to a crescendo, blending with the roar of the river. The last bend of the road was on a high bank where the sound of river the was deafening. The water spray rose high above the bank wetting the road surface. Dr. Pillai watched the stream that flowed so gently only a few months ago. The water leaped in its fury as if to swallow the trees and rocks on the bank. The white brilliance of the foam and the cascading spray covered the surface of the river. At intervals huge boulders from the collapsing banks fell into the river with mighty explosions. The river was like an enormous dragon rushing forth through the dark valley, spreading terror and destruction.

Dr. Pillai was greatly respected in the Tibetan labour camp. It was not so much his medical competence that had earned the respect, but his good fortune that the Tibetans had remained almost completely unexposed to modern medicine, and drugs like penicillin worked miraculously on them. He was called Doctor Lama in the Tibetan camp, and was an object of special affection. His introspective nature, which made him diffident in his official surroundings, found a release with these people. He was always invited to their communal festivals. In an atmosphere of affectionate welcome, he overcame his self-consciousness and participated in the festivities with an unexpected exuberance. It was as if their easy acceptance of him and the stimulation of their heady wine broke through the repressions in his mind.

"Doctor Lama," the forty-five-year-old wife of the labour mate recognized him.

"Doctor Saheb," Doma Pasang and her friends who danced near the fire surrounded the doctor. The beat of the music, the *chaang*, and the smiling eyes of the dancers struck chords of gaiety in the doctor's mind.

"What is the celebration for?" But without getting an answer, he was drawn into the circle of dancers. His self-conscious hesitations were swept away by the eager exhortations to keep in step with Doma.

The *chaang* boiled in a big kettle near the fire. Doma's husband filled a large glass for the doctor. Six months ago, Doma had a miraculous escape. Slipping from the narrow road, she had nearly gone down the depth of the narrow gorge. Luckily, her clothes got caught in the branches of a tree on the sheer slope fifty feet below the road level. Her husband then rescued her by swinging down on a rubber pipe of the air compressor. Many injections and drips of glucose pulled her through the coma caused by the loss of blood and broken bones. The Tibetans watched the glucose drip as if it was her last link with life.

Dr Pillai had often thought that the Tibetan zest for life was based on their easy acceptance of the changing circumstances of life. Perhaps it was this attitude that kept them happy in all situations. In the gravest of circumstances, they could find humour to lighten their mood. In the deepening night, the doctor could not have said if it was the dance, glory of the moonlight, or the faces of dancers laughing in the light of the leaping fire, that had imbued a gay spirit in him. He wondered what had gone wrong with the cultural patterns of his life which were the result of centuries-old traditions. Somehow they did not bring spontaneous enjoyment from the simple things of life and reduced everything to lifeless rituals.

"Doctor Saheb," the voices zoomed. It was the stimulation of the *chaang* mixed with the smell of meat roasting on fire, and the intoxicating closeness of young dancers. He felt alive and not so alone. The valley had come to life with vibrant dance and music. The humid breeze blowing through the trees was heavy with its contact with wet leaves. It was like the voluptuous embrace of a mature woman. High up, near the snow-covered peaks, the air had a crisp freshness, like the inexperienced simplicity of the surrender of a young girl.

In the bright moonlight, the silvery mountain peaks rose majestically far above the jungle and human life, into the beatitude of a spiritual world, as if they were the sentinels guarding the heavens. They stood timeless and untouched by the past, future, or the present—eternal in the continuance of the world order, symbolizing a combination of the physical and spiritual energy. They smiled on the frolics of men to say, "Play to your heart's content. It is all a game which has gone by and which is still to come. A play of endless variety."

The flood came at three in the morning. Anguished cries of men and women were drowned in the deluge of the high wave. Nobody saw the full extent of the wave, or perhaps no one remained to describe its enormity. At dawn, the wave had hurtled several miles down in the Menshithang valley where the span of the river was much wider.

Further down, the river passed through a steep gorge. Perhaps the flood water had remained at a high level at Menshithang for a long time because of this obstruction. The frequent explosions of the collapsing rocks of the narrow gorge, crackling and falling under the monstrous power of the flood water, filled the hearts of the victims of the flood at Menshithang with terror.

"Saheb! Saheb!" Assistant Executive Engineer Sharma was instantaneously drawn into the electrified atmosphere of the night as soon as the loud knocking at the door of his room woke him. Outside the room, the scene was as if the sea had surged into the valley. Broken branches of trees uprooted by the flood swirled in the water-filled football field. Screams and wailing sounds rose from the tents left standing at the Tibetan Camp.

"Saheb! Saheb!"

His orderly was terrified, speechless beyond uttering the two words.

Major Sadashiv's room was unoccupied. The doctor was also not in his room.

"Major Saheb up! Gone up!"

"Call Subedar Saheb!" Sharma shook the orderly by the shoulders to break him out of his stupefaction.

In the fading moonlight, dark shapes of men and women could be seen as they rushed to the tents of the labour camp, in desperate attempts to salvage their belongings. Two of the trucks parked on the road below the Offices' Mess were fully submerged. Another had rolled over on its side, with its tarpaulin cover still visible above the gushing water. A few jawans pushed another truck towards the high ground. In the bright headlights of the truck, Sharma saw that the high ground was completely dry as there was no rain.

"Jai Hind, Saab." Subedar Banta Singh came to report that the flood water level was well below the pioneer's barracks. "Two pioneers and a driver sleeping in one of the submerged trucks are missing. The driver of the overturned truck is seriously injured. He has been taken to the medical inspection room."

Both sentries on duty at the outpost near the football field were missing. Perhaps they had dozed off, and got caught in the flood. There was no report of any other casualty or missing person from the camp.

"More than half the Tibetans have been washed away, Saab," Banta Singh said. "Several of them were sleeping around the football field after their mela."

"Sharma! Get the Tibetans up here from their camp. Rush on! Use the trucks."

Suddenly, Major Sadashiv's voice boomed out of the darkness beyond the beams of the truck's headlight.

The second wave of the flood was five feet higher. The crashing sound of the rolling boulders and the uprooted trees echoed through the valley. Sharma saw the approaching wall of water a few minutes after the trucks had stopped near the Tibetans' camp. The foaming water of the second wave travelled above the surface of the water already swirling in the football field. The waters surged forth, roaring and crushing everything under its terrible might. It was like the line of ancient warriors charging forward to attack the enemy with loud battle cries.

Many people at the camp saw the full fury of the second wave in its rush across the valley. The first wave was not seen by them, but no one missed the terrifying impact and destruction spread by the second wave. Watching the fury of the approaching water, Sharma felt for a few moments that the force of rushing water would wash all of them away along with the vehicles. However, finally the water-level did not rise above the tyres of the last truck, and like an island, a part of the Tibetan camp remained a few feet above the water level.

No one could understand how so many Tibetans were drowned in the second wave which raised the water level only by five feet. But those who were present at Menshithang on that terrible night did not understand how so many of them could save themselves.

The Court of Inquiry appointed to investigate the drowning of three men of the rescue party that had gone to the Tibetan camp with their vehicles, had finally laid the blame on Sharma's inexperience. Major Sadashiv's order to Sharma to send these people on this mission was also considered responsible for the mishap. Subedar

Banta Singh held an opinion to the contrary, though on account of his limitations of self-expression, he was not able to say so clearly in his official evidence before the Court of Inquiry.

After his experience of shifting the injured and the dead to the Medical Inspection room in the early light of dawn, Sharma could not think clearly about the matter. But undoubtedly Major Sadashiv had risen considerably in his estimation. He did not understand at all, how the characteristically easy-going relaxed mind of Major Sadashiv could quickly propel himself to climb up to the signal centre situated above the Officers' Mess. It was his warning to units stationed several miles down in the valley of the approaching danger, which saved a complete platoon of the Gurkha infantry from being washed away by the flood. A few days after appearing before the Court Inquiry, Sharma was able to give a more balanced account of the events in a letter to a friend working with another unit of the Border Roads.

"After watching the wave of the flood that night, I can now imagine what the waves of the sea must be like in a storm. I feel that most of the destruction caused by the wave had resulted from the reactions which the sight of the approaching water produced in the Tibetan labour camp. A report had been received earlier in the evening that the river level had receded by one foot. After several days of rain the sky had cleared, and on hearing the report about the receding water level, everybody felt that the danger of the flood was over.

"This news had also travelled to the Tibetan labour camp. As you know, these people need only an excuse for a celebration. Dancing and music continued in the football field till late at night. The three of us had remained in the Mess till fairly late that night. I was teasing the doctor and he walked out in a fit of anger. I understand that he had also joined the orgy of the Tibetans. The strange story of the doctor is a tale by itself.

The first wave of the flood must have come at about three in the morning. I had never imagined that so much water could accumulate in the green lakes. The dancing and the music of the Tibetans had died down long before the flood arrived. But, it is their custom that after soaking themselves with *chaang* and *tumba*, the happy couples lie around the fire. They have a fairly free sex life, and on days of such festivity men and women give themselves up to their uninhibited impulses. Many of these couples, already half way to heaven, were carried off by the first wave.

Those of them who could save themselves from the first wave, scrambled up to awaken people in the tents pitched on higher ground. Just as the tragic gravity of the situation dawned on these people, the terrifying fury of the second wave swept them off. There was a stampede of terror-stricken men, women, and children running in all directions for safety. Our trucks reached there about the same time. I had told the drivers to keep the engines running and the headlights on. The flood water surged forward with such a menacing roar that for a few moments I felt that all of us would be completely overwhelmed by it. Similar terrifying thoughts must also have arisen in the minds of the Tibetans. Many of them had already suffered from the fury of the first wave. In the dark terror of the rising water, our trucks and their powerful headlights must have appeared as beacons of human strength in defiance of the forces of nature. In this situation, as soon as the trucks stopped, the entire stampede wasdirected towards them.

I have never seen a more terrible sight. On one side was the foaming wrath of the flood, and on the other was the mad human wave, pushing, stampeding, and climbing over each other. I did not know that most Tibetans slept without any clothes. In the streaming headlights of the trucks naked figures of men and women running from their camp could be seen slipping down and being trampled over. It was as if in their desperation to cling to the last link with life, men had lowered themselves to an animal level. I hope never to see such a terrible scene again."

It was also an unusual day in the personal world of Dr. Pillai. After being found missing from his room at three in the morning, the doctor was seen limping about the medical inspection room at day break, attending to the injured. Late in the evening, after attending to innumerable patients he was removed to the Base Military Hospital by the last flight of the helicopter, delirious with high fever. And it was a completely changed doctor who returned to the camp after a month at the hospital. He had undergone a complete psychic transformation.

Recollections of his gradual intoxication, of the rhythms and the quickening beat of the dance, were buried deep in the layers of his memory. The first contact with a woman's body, excitement, the culmination, was a part of an upheaval of which he could trace neither the beginning nor the end.

There was a storm in his mind in which there were no specific shapes; only the floating memories of touch, taste, and smell. Before his intoxicated body could awaken from his dreams to full consciousness of the flood, he was knocked unconscious by an uprooted tree. Thereafter, it was only the force of his life line which caused him to get entangled in the branches of a tree jutting into the flood waters, which saved him from being carried down the river with the second wave. When he came around, his entire body was full of scratches and he had a terrible pain in his legs. He straggled back to the camp through the river bed which was strewn with dead and dying human bodies. It was a traumatic shock after the voluptuous dancers of the previous night. Physically it was impossible for him to return to the camp with his injuries. But some extra rational inner forces stimulated by the vision of the dead around him propelled him on. And it was the same mysterious subconscious energy, which kept him on his feet attending to the injured the whole day until he was evacuated by the last trip of the helicopter in a state of total exhaustion.

Major Sadashiv could not resist mentioning him in a letter he wrote to his wife soon after the doctor had returned from the Base Military Hospital.

"... Newspapers have published reports about last month's flood in which many people died. The Medical Officer of our unit was also seriously injured. He has just returned after a month's treatment in the hospital. He seems to be a completely changed man. Earlier he used to behave just like a boy..."

In sharp contrast to Major Sadashiv's brief and simple letter, Assistant Executive Engineer Sharma had expressed his opinion about the Major's conduct on the night of the flood at the end of his long letter to his friend.

".... After working under Major Sadashiv for the past several months, I had thought that I understood the mental frame of a 'Passed Over' Major. If there is a certainty at a fairly young age of retiring at the same rank and working under your former subordinates, what else can you except from a man? But after the events of that night, I have been compelled to think about it again.

"I just cannot understand how the Major found the presence of mind and the promptness that immediately on getting the news of the flood he rushed to the signal centre to inform units further down the river, and also decided that the left-over people in the Tibetan camp must be evacuated to high ground. For this decision, it was essential for him to have made a correct assessment of the possibility of a second wave and the situations that might develop from it.

"If we had not sent our trucks to the Tibetan labour camp that night, perhaps none of them would have survived. It was observed later on that the stampede was started by the arrival of our trucks. But was there any guarantee that the second wave would not be many feet higher than it was, and that there would not be a third wave? Under those circumstances what would have been the reaction of those terror-stricken marooned people? At least our trucks saved two-thirds of them for a certainty...."

Late in the afternoon, two helicopters flew several sorties to evacuate the wounded to the Base Military Hospital. But Major Sadashiv's life had returned to its steady pace long before that. The truth is that except for the initial forty minutes, there was no change in his expressionless countenance. He did not even realize that when the wounded were being brought to the camp, how reassuring was his unexcited neutral face for everyone. If Sharma, or anyone else, had asked him how he found that presence of mind in those crucial initial minutes, he would probably not even have understood the question. It is possible that under the month long tension about the probability of a flood, his subconscious mind had worked on many imaginary eventualities. But it would perhaps be best to discard all speculation on this, and leave it to the immense mystery of the human mind.

Teju's Letter

"Oon!.. ...Oon!..Mummy Oon!... my Mummy! Oon! ...Oon!... Mummy! Oon!...Oon!..." The 15 month-old-little boy was whining for his mother. Teju who was eleven years old and was employed to look after the little boy, had brought him to the roof. He got so irritated and fed up by the ten-minute long constant whining that he slapped the little boy. This converted the whine into a shriek and loud crying.

Nervously, Teju looked all around. But there was no one else on the roof. On the floor below, Sahib had finished his lunch and had already gone to his bedroom for his afternoon nap. It was still more than an hour for Bibiji, i.e. Mummy, to come back after her shopping. A worried Teju looked at the little boy helplessly and then picked him up to swing him in his lap in an effort to quieten him.

His efforts, however, led to the little boy crying even louder. Hopelessly harassed, Teju put the little boy down to sit on the floor.

A few clouds floated in the sky in the late afternoon. Across the road from the house, yellow crops of mustard growing in open fields that stretched right up to the river, were waving with the afternoon breeze. To the right, in a village that had survived the onslaught of the growing big city, a few cows tied to their pegs comfortably were chewing cud. With the arrival of the domestic dog on the roof, the little boy had forgotten his crying to play with him.

Standing close to the parapet in the now peaceful afternoon on the roof, Teju's eyes filled with tears. Far away, beyond the distant horizon, near the dark clouds, it must be raining in his village .....

Drops of rain must be leaking through the tiled roof of the house. His mother would be cooking the evening meal while attending to his kid sister. Rain drops getting pushed into the hearth by gusts of rain must have filled the house with smoke. Teju's mind travelled far away, beyond the yellow mustard crops, across the river, though he had promised his father and mother that he would not return for at least six months.

His father had said, "Your mother says your heart is not in your studies. Now you have grown up. Go and work in the big town. You will see the world. You'll become a man".

Teju pulled out a green pencil from the box of coloured pencils of the little boy's play things, and started writing a letter:

Bapu,

I have now completed three months service here. Bibiji has gone out since morning. The baby boy is here, playing with the dog. It's a wicked dog. It bites me.

Yesterday, Bibiji hit me. She didn't give me any food. A glass tumbler had broken as it slipped from my hands.

I will come back home after three months. Now I will work hard to study. Doctor Saab comes to the house in his car. He gets a lot of money. I will become a doctor. Bibijis of big towns remain ill.

They don't do any work.

There are three servants in the house. Bibiji does not cook food. A bearer washes the plates with soap. Sahib goes to his office in a car. Bibiji goes to the market. She brings home more and more new things every day. She changes her clothes many times a day. She does not wear torn saris. I will bring a new sari for my mother from the bazaar. Also, a plastic panty for my little sister. Then, mother's sari will not get dirty.

Saheb and Bibiji read newspapers. They sit in the big room and talk to people. They go to the club. They kiss the little boy before going to sleep. The little boy sleeps with the ayah. When there is no one in the house, the ayah beats the little boy.

I will bring my little sister a frock. Also, a big dog she can play with. When she grows up, she will be a Bibiji. I will become a doctor and treat her illnesses.

I wake up early in the morning. As the sun rises above the river, I take the little boy out on rounds in a cart. There are two vehicles in this house. A small red one, and a big imported car. I will bring my little sister a red car. One car is enough for one child. But how will a car run on the unpaved roads of our village?

Bibiji wakes up after Saheb leaves for his office. Before going out shopping, she sits in front of a table with a big mirror. There are many coloured bottles on that table. I will bring coloured bottles for mother. Then mother will also pile her hair high, wear a new sari, and go shopping.

Bapu, I will bring you a black coat. Then, you can go to an office to work. We will live in a big town. In a new house whose roof does not leak.

The horn of a car on the road broke Teju's reverie. The boy playing with the dog had gone down. It was also time for Bibiji to be back. The dark clouds on the horizon were clearing up. Teju could not think of writing anything else in his letter. As he folded the letter to put in his pocket, he felt that something was not quite right in his letter.

In the setting sun, the slanting shadow of the house on the road became longer. The cows in the village were rising after finishing their chewing. As Teju came down from the roof to look for the little boy, his mind was much more relaxed.

★★★

The Storm

It was the beginning of March. It rained in the afternoon and fresh snow fell on the mountain tops. After the day long journey on winding hill roads the bus was now running at full speed on the straight road of the valley. Besides the conductor, only seven people were now in the bus. The two Tibetan woman who entered the bus in the morning and were constantly sick on the winding mountain roads, now lay back exhausted. The man accompanying them slept with his elbows resting on the front seat. A village woman from Kangra, sat on the seat behind the driver with a child in her lap. She kept talking non-stop to her husband. On the opposite seat, an Englishman with a thick tangled beard looked very tired. He had slept through most of his journey since the early afternoon.

At the end of the second row a man on my right sat next to the window. He had remained wide awake the whole time. After the rain stopped he often stretched his neck out of the moving bus several times to take photographs of the mountains. The rest of the time, he either looked out of the window or stared at other passengers in the bus. At times he would mutter and smile to himself. His eyes had a curious glint and he kept giving me furtive looks. He wore a brown coat and a black beret. Late in the afternoon when the village woman from Kangra suckled her child, he shamelessly stared at her full firm breasts. For some time he sat with his bent head supported by his elbows, and his body trembled as if he had spasms. Whenever he noisily cleared his throat, the Englishman turned around to talk to him.

Both of them had come into the bus in the early afternoon. The Englishman looked exhausted even at that time. The other man appeared disturbed and his face was tense. I was curious about him but something held me back from starting a conversation.

The sun was setting behind the mountains. The bus ran an hour and a half behind its schedule. Suddenly a few sheep crossed the road, and the jolt of brakes woke up the drowsy Englishman. It was already dark inside the bus. The Englishman turned back and asked his companion for the time. Without answering, his companion stretched out his hand with the watch towards the Englishman. It was well past six o'clock.

"Perhaps you want to catch the evening train?" I turned towards the Englishman.

"Yes indeed." His sleep had refreshed him somewhat.

"I doubt if we will make the first train but there is a second one a little later," I said, "You should have caught the earlier bus."

"We had planned to do that," he replied glancing at his companion who was still looking out of the window, "But we got late. We had to walk ten miles on a slushy hill track."

The Tibetan women returned to normal now that the bus was no longer on the winding curves of the hilly road. They began quarrelling between themselves. The young woman from Kangra was shouting at her husband.

"Noisy women," the Englishman said.

"Yes", his companion said loudly in a strangely vibrating voice. "Women do make a lot of noise." His loud voice was so discordant that everybody's attention was diverted towards us. The Tibetan women stopped quarrelling and fell silent. The young couple from Kangra turned around to see what was the matter. The driver switched on the light inside the bus. The moon light shone on the fields on either side of the road.

The Englishman's companion had gone back to bending his head between the elbows. The Englishman was visibly embarrassed by his friend's outburst.

"Please do not mind him," the Englishman whispered to me, "he has met with a terrible misfortune. There was a calamity day before yesterday. His fiancée got drowned in the lake." His companion continued to sit with his head bent. He could obviously overhear our conversation.

"In the lake? Where? In which lake?" I could no longer contain my curiosity.

The Englishman also appeared keen to speak as if to get it all out of his system.

"Fifteen miles above Mandi there is a lake near the top of the mountain. The lake is close to the Tibetan settlement at Rewalsar. You may have heard of it," he glanced at his companion and went on. "Rewalsar is a holy place for the Tibetans. According to a legend, the local king had ordered the Tibetan saint Padma Sambhava to be burnt alive. But the oil meant to burn the saint turned into water and formed the lake. Ever since, Rewalsar has been a place of pilgrimage for Tibetans."

For the last few years it has become common to find foreigners in all sorts of peculiar places in India. Still, I was intrigued by his easy manner.

"What were you doing there?" I asked him.

"I am working on a project for the resettlement of Tibetan refugees. Many Tibetans get employed in road building works all over the mountain ranges. They leave their wives and children at Rewalsar where we run a school for them."

The lights of Pathankot city were visible now. The Englishman's companion was quietly looking out of the window. The Tibetan women were fussing with their luggage.

"How did the accident take place?" I asked.

His companion could obviously overhear us. But he sat impassively with a vacant look. It was a full moon night. The bus ran at full speed in the soft moonlight. After the cold mountain air, the mild breeze of the plains was full of a warm aroma of the ripening corn in the fields.

"It was a tragic accident," the Englishman said. "You can see how beautiful the nights are these days. Both of us were scheduled to leave Rewalsar today for a month's absence. Two days ago, his fiancée suggested a moonlight picnic on the lake. It was a clear night. But later when our party was in full swing in the middle of the lake, the clouds came up and there was a big storm. Our boat started taking in water. Perhaps the big waves or our frantic movement in the boat accidentally knocked out the boat's plug."

"Is it a big lake?" I asked.

"No. But while the rest of us jumped out to swim ashore, he and his fiancée could not swim at all and they clung to the boat, which finally did not sink. When we returned in another boat, there was no trace of her. The water was cold and her hand must have slipped. He was also unconscious but taking off his shirt he had tied himself to the boat."

The corn fields were now left behind. The bus now ran on the well lit city roads.

"In the morning some of her clothes were found floating in the lake. The corpse came up late in the afternoon. It was cremated the same evening."

The bus neared the stand. After a minute's silence he continued, "She was an extraordinary woman. A combination of such good looks and intelligence is rare."

"But what led both of them to go to Rewalsar and undertake this work? What could be the reason?" I could not understand at all.

"Reason!" He gave me an odd look. "It is difficult to understand why people act in certain ways. Every day I myself seem to find different reasons for my presence here."

The bus had reached the stand. The Kangra couple were taking down the luggage through the entry door.

He went on, "Things do not always happen the way we expect them to, nor is there only one approach to everything. Human actions spring from all sorts of conscious and unconscious motivations. People act and then learn to bear the consequences of their actions with fortitude and inner strength they possess."

It was a coincidence that after meeting my friends in town when I reached the station and found my place in the train, I saw the same brown coat and black beret lying on the opposite berth. As there was still some time before the train left, after depositing my luggage in the compartment, I decided to stroll along the platform. It was then that I noticed the Englishman's companion at the opposite end of the platform. I waved to him but he did not respond. Perhaps he was completely absorbed in himself. He was a tall man and was walking up and down the platform with his hands clenched behind his back.

He climbed into the train as it started moving and lay down on his berth. It was a four-berth compartment and the upper two berths were unoccupied. I was unable to make out whether his face was really pale or only appeared so in the faint light of the compartment. I wanted to talk to him but we remained silent. He lay on his berth staring at the light on the ceiling.

"Is your English friend also on this train?" I tried to initiate a conversation.

He remained silent for some time and then cleared his throat noisily. "No! He managed to find accommodation on the earlier train."

His words seemed controlled but the voice was often choked and broken. He continued to lie on his berth, and I could not think of anything else to say. Soon I dropped off to sleep.

When I woke up the train had stopped at a station. It was ten o'clock and the waiter from the restaurant car was taking orders for breakfast the next morning.

I normally find it difficult to sleep in a train, more so when the lights are on. He was awake and sitting up.

"If you want me to switch off the lights, I will do so," he said looking at me.

"Not really," I pulled out a magazine from my briefcase, I am not feeling sleepy."

The train pulled out of the platform. The engine was puffing to pick up speed.

"Your friend told me. I am very sorry," I said. He had a book which he tried to read unsuccessfully for some time. When he stretched his hands, I noticed that they were trembling.

"Have you ever seen a murderer?" There was a strange glint in his eyes. "She was not my fiancée. But that was what she used to say at times. I killed her."

He stopped talking. There was total silence in the compartment. I was dumbstruck. Perhaps the shock of the tragedy had affected his mind. I thought of changing to another compartment at the next station. In the silence that followed, both of us made futile attempts to read our books.

"If you wish to sleep, I can switch off the lights," he said again.

"No, thank you, I am not at all sleepy", I replied. I did not relish the possibility of darkness in the compartment.

"Excuse me, If you are really not sleepy, may I take some of your time", he coughed to clear his throat, "I have heard that Christians confess for absolution. If you do not mind, perhaps telling you about this tragedy may help me get over it."

Through the train's windows one could see a line of small hills beyond the corn fields. Flecks of white clouds had clustered around the moon. A cool breeze blew which came in through the window. He sat still on his berth and kept looking out of the window.

"Roop was only nineteen when I met her for the first time. Her father taught at the University and a few months before our examination he started holding extra classes every Sunday at his residence. Then I discovered a distant relationship with her mother and that led to my frequent visits to her house. In those days she was a plain and simple girl and no one could have imagined that she would change so drastically. Her music tutor came to teach her the sitar in the evenings and occasionally I went in to listen. This was the beginning of our friendship."

He kept quiet. Soot from the engine was blew in. I pushed up the window pane.

He bent forward and said, "Do you believe that a man incapable of fierce hatred is also incapable of deep love? Is it true that love and hate are only two facets of the same emotion? Do they not frequently merge into each other? I would like to know what love is and why people pursue it?"

"Why don't you also push up the window pane on your side?" I said. But he ignored my question.

"I continued to visit her house and we met quite often. Every girl is attractive at nineteen but I slowly realized that she also had a depth of mind though she was still quite young and could get moulded in any direction. Her mother was old fashioned but she trusted me. Perhaps she had not realized that her daughter was no longer a child.

"A few weeks before my examinations, I became aware that we were not at ease with each other. Apart from the normal attraction for a young girl, I had never specifically thought about her. I realized that the tension came from her. You know that all sorts of sentimental ideas enter the human mind silently and gain ascendancy only at certain moments. Conscious reasoning may lead in a certain direction but slowly the drives of the subconscious mind make inroads, and the final action often strays far from the logical path.

"I was aware of the tension. She did not say anything but I could feel the undercurrents. We did not have any physical relationship between us though I knew that if I wanted I could take the initiative. But I did not feel deeply about her and I continued to behave normally as before. At times when my ego pushed me, I would rebuke myself, but I could not stop going to her house. I sensed that my indifferent attitude would increase the intensity of her feelings. But I refused to understand this clearly. I convinced myself that I was behaving properly and had done nothing to take improper advantage of the situation. I did not let this subject ever come up in our conversation."

He bent forward, shut the window, and kept staring at me. But it appeared that his eyes had really turned to an inward search. He was lost in the maze of his mind.

"Do you think I should have taken our relationship to a physical level?"

I was not sure whether he even expected a reply from me. I said, "But you did not love her."

"I want to know what love means?" His voice was suddenly excited and loud. "How can you talk of love so simply?"

I was somewhat taken aback. "I only said that a physical relationship without feelings would amount to a lustful exploitation."

"Lust!" His loud voice boomed in the compartment "What is the meaning of lust? What do you understand about exploitation? For a small physical act what big words we use. Have you ever thought about mental exploitation?"

He was silent for some time before continuing, "My examinations were about to finish and I was due to return home. There was no change in the situation. On the day of my departure, I went to take leave of her family. She was in her room and I said goodbye from the door. She did not reply. We stood silently for some time.

Many years have elapsed now but I remember her face as it was on that day. There was a long row of trees outside her room. 'Goodbye', she said after a long pause. It was the beginning of May and the Amaltas trees were full of yellow blossoms. I remained silent, and then I turned and came away from her room. It is strange that the poignance of that day had slipped from my memory for a long time. In later years, perhaps a search for the inner inter-relationship of events brought up the picture vividly from the subconscious depths of my mind."

The train rushed along the platform of a wayside station without stopping. The reverberations from a goods train on the next track shook the compartment.

"Can you tell me the difference between a physical and a mental relationship? If there is no pregnancy what difference does it make? Are these not complementary relations? Don't you agree that physical relations keep the human mind on an even keel? Do physical contacts not prevent the aberrations of a platonic relationship? If the intellect is considered supreme what is the justification for giving so much importance to a mere physical act?"

"Many years must have elapsed since you met her the first time", I asked, wanting to change the subject.

"Yes, it is about seven years now," he said, "That was my first year at the university. Soon, I got busy with settling down to my new situations of life, and drifted away from old relationships.

"Four years passed. And one day I suddenly met Roop again when I had gone on leave to her town and was crossing a street. I almost did not recognize her.

'Aha! You do not even remember me!' she said taking off her dark glasses. It was her all right, though she had changed a lot. Her body had filled up and she was dressed with a deliberate simplicity. Instead of the innocent simplicity of earlier years there was a clever elegance. The immature and inexperienced girl of four years ago was transformed.

"How come you are here?" I asked.

"What did you think?" Her wheatish complexion stood out against the white sari. "You just disappeared without a trace."

I could just stare at her.

I went to their house the next day. Her father had retired and they lived in a suburb, seven or eight miles from the centre of town. Her mother was ill and father had aged. Roop was a teacher in a local college since last year.

"She wants to take up a good job with the government. She thinks teaching is a waste of time," her father said.

"Ambitious!" I said looking at her, "Government jobs are glamorous only from a distance. The bureaucracy attracts only the mediocre".

Her father laughed "No, the real reason is that the father's profession never seems attractive to their children."

"Have you given up your sitar?" I asked,

She sat on a chair opposite me, playing with her necklace. It was impossible not to feel the intoxication of her proximity.

"You have not given up your old habit of lecturing," she said, "It's you who should have been a teacher."

"Round pegs in square holes," I replied. "You have become so clever. When you join government service, you will get even cleverer."

Her mother was inside the house. She asked about my parents and complained that I had forgotten them. I promised to come and see them again before my leave ended.

"Roop came to see me off to the taxi stand. We arranged to meet the next day. In the seven days left of my vacation we met several times. And I realized how pleasant it was to be with her. People do not think when they are happy. Not of the present, nor of the future, nor even of the past. They do not even realize that they are happy.

"We did not talk about anything in particular. Roop had learnt the art of not letting the conversation steer beyond a level. She was conscious of her beauty and well-versed in spinning her charms effortlessly. Often I wondered how a simple girl could change so much in four years."

The train was nearing a junction. The number of tracks multiplied in proportion to the size of the station. Soon there were many tracks lit up by the searchlights in the yard. The steam hissing from the engines in the yard was a brilliant white under the flood lights. With an increase in the rattling noise of the rails he had stopped his narration. When the train stopped, the lights from the platform illuminated his face. His tension seemed somewhat relaxed. But his eyes still had a vacant look.

"Do you agree that there should be harmony between the body and the intellect?", he suddenly asked.

"I don't understand you," I replied.

But he ignored me and went on, "If one's mental processes and intellectual growth outstep the physical experience of life, an imbalance is inevitable. Do you realize how slowly the earth changes? Look at this plain land of corn fields. It has remained level and smooth for centuries since it was formed thousands of years ago by the silting of rivers. Major changes in this landscape take place only through earthquakes or volcanic eruptions. You may not agree but the human mind also works in the same way, I think that is the law of nature."

"What are you saying?" I was surprised by what he said.

"Yes! I am right. You don't understand a thing," he shouted almost hysterically.

Then he kept quiet as the train moved out of the station.

"Please forgive me, I am so preoccupied with myself that I lose control," he said.

Outside, the moonlight fell softly on the fields. It was getting cold and I pulled up the blanket to cover my feet. After the apology he kept staring out of the window.

"I do not know what happened to her in those four years. I only learnt later that she had tried to commit suicide twice. Her parents dismissed these incidents as mere accidents. She also refused to talk about them. Gradually, I realized how determined she could be. Beneath her charming manner there was a firm protective shell which did not allow much probing. Outwardly she was a beautiful happy young woman full of life and only slowly could I sense the turmoil deep inside her.

"Two more years passed. Whenever I went to her town we would meet. We kept up a correspondence. And we rebuilt our friendship on a new plane. I cannot really explain our relationship. Could we have called it love? But love is a strange feeling and it does not seem possible to understand it. It is perhaps best not to talk about it. There was a definite longing for a physical relationship. But our intellectual complexities and mental inhibitions did not permit a mutual surrender. We did not give in to our natural impulses as two normal people would perhaps have done."

"What are you saying? How can you consider such irresponsible behaviour normal?" I could not restrain myself.

"Such foolish inhibitions destroyed our lives." Suddenly his voice turned loud and sharp, "Have you ever noticed that among animals the first sign of attraction between a male and a female is physical contact? If one violates the rules of the sensual world with intellectual concerns, is it not natural that resulting repressions would destroy one's mental stability?"

Aware of his excitement he kept quiet for a while.

"Whatever else we may have felt for each other at different times we always retained a deep-seated mutual respect. In our relationship this was the only thing I always felt sure about. I was aware that off and on she entered into and broke off relationships with many men. I am sure that she had also heard many such stories about me. But, perhaps, unknown to us there was an empathy which bound our subconscious minds. Perhaps it was because of this that our relationship persisted. But on an emotional level we could not trust ourselves with each other. What a strange affair it was."

He was silent. And then suddenly he asked, "What do you understand by education and knowledge?"

"I… do not know … what you mean," I replied hesitatingly, not knowing what sort of answer was expected from me. "I think… the important thing is to understand one's own mind."

"Ah! ha!" His sharp voice rang out in the compartment. "How easily you say these things! How easy it is to talk neutrally! Have you ever tried to understand yourself under the stress of emotional turmoil? What is knowledge? Do you think one can gain knowledge by reading books? Does that not confuse one's mind? Don't you think that life can only be understood by living it firsthand".

It was two o'clock. I poured some coffee from my thermos and offered him a cup. We sipped our coffee in the silence of our compartment. He had covered himself with a blanket. His face softened. Perhaps his tension had eased.

"Last year I was transferred to her town. I was aware that Roop entered into frequent short term affairs. It is not difficult for an attractive young woman to have such relationships. They were obviously a substitute for something deeper she had missed in her life. It would have been apparent to any dispassionate observer that such relationships could only add to her emotional confusion. But it was impossible to talk to Roop on this subject. She would never let the topic arise. And if ever the talk bordered on this subject, she would act completely innocent. I never believed that she was unaware of what was happening. After all the game was her own creation. But when one wants to disbelieve something even after seeing it clearly, perhaps one gradually loses the faculty of even seeing it."

"I do not understand how in spite of seeing it all so clearly you continued to be deeply attached to her", I said.

"I have asked myself this question hundreds of times", he replied. "You may find it difficult to believe but I could never find her false. We never lost our basic respect for each other. Perhaps we had foolishly looked at the situation purely in a celebral manner and made no demands on each other. But in spite of such emotional confusions, we always felt that at some deep inner level we were very close to each other."

"I must say this is most peculiar," I could not refrain from reacting.

"One day Roop came to my house", ignoring my remarks and seeming to be completely lost in his world of fantasies, he went on, "It was the end of April. After the heat of the day there was a cool breeze in the evening. I was sitting in the lawn reading a book. Roop arrived unexpectedly and went into the house. We had not met for a few days. I picked up my book and followed her. Roop lay on the sofa with her face covered with her hands. She was weeping. I sat quietly beside her. After a while she looked up. Her face was smeared by *kajal* and her hair was dishevelled. I thought how beautiful she was without the embellishments of make-up. I bent down and kissed her. Yet only a moment afterwards, I realized that this trifling physical surrender was only a temporary matter of passivity on her part. The line of mistrust between us remained deep as ever before.

"She sat up on the sofa. Her face was flushed with tears. She said, "Do you think I am a bad person? Why do I hurt people? I do not want to trouble anyone. I do not want to cry."

There could be no answer to such questions, They could only be asked and answered by each one internally. Perhaps it was a matter of one's experiences and mental discipline. It was obvious that one of her short affairs had ended badly. There was no point in my asking for details. More than anyone else she herself must be aware of the futility of such relationships. Even seeing the absurdity of this situation, it was impossible for me not to sympathize with Roop's misery."

"Then, your sentiments must really have been a kind of pity," I could not help commenting.

"Pity!" His voice rose to a high pitch again, "What a strange thing to say! Pity is such a shallow and ludicrous sentiment. I think it reflects poorly on both the giver and the receiver. What could be the meaning of pity in the context of our situation?"

"Roop did not need pity from anyone, he continued, "I knew that the next day she would again be the self-confident playful woman, proud of her beauty. In spite of all such aberrations, I always admired her zest for life."

"It is strange", I said "that knowing such aspects of her conduct you accepted the situation as it was. After all, it was a grossly irresponsible and immature behaviour."

"You are right!", he said. For a long time there was total silence in the compartment. I looked at my watch. It was past three-thirty. When he spoke again his voice was very soft. "Since I am the narrator, the story is bound to get one-sided. But I cannot close my eyes to my own acts of irresponsibility. Often a man realizes his weakness only after the situation is already beyond redemption."

"Feelings of self-respect and self-confirmation manifest themselves in a peculiar manner in emotional relationships. You will appreciate that self-preservation is one of the strongest human drives. But there is no defence against emotional insecurity because there is no set way to overcome it. I could not remain unaffected by such pressures though I saw the situation with clarity from time to time. But there is a world of a difference between analysis of a situation and one's ability to act in accordance with them in the turbulence of life."

He continued, "In my strange relationship with Roop many complications arose because of my actions. In physical matters it is easy to rectify one's mistakes, but in emotional life things are not so easy. Our ego also adds to the feelings of emotional distrust and prevents any act of surrender.."

The train had stopped at a wayside station. Day break was still a few hours away. On the almost empty platform two railway clerks wandered around with blankets wrapped around them to face the cold night air. I peeped out of the window to look for a tea seller. But there was no one in sight besides the two clerks.

"I met John Hardy about six months ago", he went on, "Do you remember him? The Englishman who was with me in the bus. He worked with Tibetan refugees for the last year and a half and wanted assistance from the government to set up an industrial centre to promote Tibetan handicrafts. A common friend introduced him to me saying that John had given up a lucrative job in London to find peace of mind in India. "John Hardy is a peculiar character," the friend told me, "he could not get on with any of the welfare organizations involved with Tibetans. Finally, he traced the remote Tibetan settlement of Riwalsar not reached by any of the relief organizations. He has converted to Buddhism, and is now running a school for Tibetan children."

"My friend's narration got me interested and I met John Hardy several times. Normally I am not impressed by people who take to strange ways and change their religion in search of peace. But I found a serene calmness in him which suggested that he had perhaps found a way to find his peace of mind. He told me about his school and his experiences with Tibetans. Roop also met him a few times and enthusiastically enquired about his work.

And then in a moment of excitement she declared that she was wasting her life aimlessly and would really like to go up to John's school to teach Tibetan children."

He stopped for a while, searching for something in his mind, and he said, "You will perhaps agree that high ideals of sacrifice and charity often take root in people's minds when they are struggling to escape their inner problems. It is like a dose of a patented medicine which can cure all diseases. The foolishness of such actions defies my understanding. Why does the human mind get out of control so easily? Why do we fool ourselves with such actions?

"In those days my relationship with Roop had reached such an unhealthy state that the emotional tension was becoming unbearable. I had begun to think that perhaps the best solution was to sever all ties with her completely. But the human mind is so wayward and unpredictable that even in such an unbearable situation, it cannot give up its wishful hopes. It is unable to reach decisions which the rational faculties would easily choose. It was in such a frame of mind that I decided to take Roop to John's mountain retreat for a few days."

He coughed to clear his throat and continued, "John Hardy's school consisted of three thatched huts which stood in a clearing below the hill top. The lake was some distance away and it was fairly large. A row of weeping willows stood on its shore and the drooping branches of the trees floated near the edge of the lake water.

The lake was encircled by a footpath on which we went for long walks every evening. On the other side of the lake was a Tibetan gompa and behind it were the shops and houses of Riwalsar. On one side of the lake was an island with many pine trees. The island was covered with pine needles whose russet colour stood out against the blue lake. On the other side of the hill, beyond a wide misty valley were the mountains of perennial snow. In the clear mountain air of early mornings the snow shone a brilliant white."

"Yes, your friends mentioned the place yesterday," I said, "Did you stay there for a long time?"

"Not really, I was there for fifteen days the first time, and a month on my next visit. And this was my third trip", he said. "Have you ever known the spell of the mountains? I think human life is intrinsically tuned to a close relationship with elements no matter how far may we drift from nature and get engrossed in our man made mechanical world. It is perhaps because of this that experiencing the beauty of nature brings serenity to human life.

"John Hardy had lived there for a year and a half. Often we went to the island in the lake in a small boat and talked for hours. He told me about his past, and how he found a new life for himself living with the Tibetans. In their way of life he found a simple harmony of work, religion, sex, and death. Life flowed with a balance that has been lost in the humdrum of modern civilization where men distort their lives by compartmentalizing them in several parts. There is no organic relationship between thoughts, emotions, and the physical aspects of life. John told me that he intended to marry a Tibetan girl and adopt their way of life permanently.

He also spent time every day to learn the Tibetan script. Watching him immersed in his new life in the quadrangle of the Buddhist gompa every morning, I could not help envying the bliss he had found in circumstances so strange and remote from those of his earlier life.

"I spoke to Roop about John Hardy. I told her about the Buddhist gompa which was full of yellow and red-robed Lamas. A Lamassery was attached to the gompa where the six-year-old young Lamas sat in long rows wearing their shining yellow robes, chanting mantras on all Sundays amidst occasional beating of drums. And how the tiny eyes of young Lamas were full of mischief as they joked between themselves when the old Lamas were not looking. I told her about the calm mood of the place and the sense of peace which pervaded the atmosphere.

"It is all an escape from life", Roop had said. But when I returned from Rewalsar the second time, she said that she would like to go there once herself."

He remained silent for some time before continuing, "It occurred to me that there was a change in Roop's manner. Perhaps she had felt that I was moving away from her. Often we do not care about things within our easy reach but start hankering after them when we feel them slipping away from us."

It was four-thirty in the morning. The lights in the compartment were switched off from the mains. We sat quietly in the darkness for some time. The first rays of daylight were beginning to appear in the eastern sky. After a long pause when my companion spoke again his voice had become very unbalanced.

"She came to Riwalsar. But why did she have to come? Can you understand what prompted her? The water in the lake was blue but it was jet black at night. In the darkness of the night you could see the white boat only when there was thunder and lightning. How lovely her bare body had looked when her sari slipped! How it thundered! What a lot of lightning there was! The water was so cold and I was burning. Man is such a crazy animal."

I kept quiet.

He went on. "She came with me. Why did I not stop her? But I had encouraged her myself. And I had thought that she would never come. When did she ever keep her promises? But she wanted to disturb the world where I had found peace. Peace! What a terrible word it is. Do you know what it means? Just to fool yourself! Do you know the peace of the graveyard?

"She was a bitch. She was my fiancée. At least she often said so. Tibetan children of the school became so fond of her. She looked beautiful. And her beauty was supplemented by the beauty of the mountains. What game had she come to play? Do you think anyone knows what one does? Do you know what John Hardy was doing? Poor John! A strange game. And we are mere puppets. Not masters of our destiny. Who can blame Roop? She did what she did. And I believed what I could. It was all a lie, a terrible lie. Nothing is true, everything is a lie. It is all a farce.

"But I could not tolerate her behaviour towards John. God alone knows what she was up to. Do you think she knew? Did John know? No woman should appear beautiful to a man. It is vulgar. What does beauty mean? Our bodies are so beautiful and our minds so awful. But I am lying. Our minds are beautiful but they are also so ugly. It is horrible!

"It was a matter of only one day. Do you hear? Just one day. Ah! how well I knew why Roop was doing what she was doing. Just one more day more! How well I understood her! But who understands anything in a live situation? Who understands moods of flesh and blood? The moonlight was so beautiful. How I hate everything beautiful! The moonlight was so beautiful. When we were pulling the boat. And when Roop was singing. I did not even think about John. My whirlwind had come much before the storm. When did the storm come? How easily did the boat plug come off! So loose! To come off with just one pull! Poor John! But I really did not think about him at all. Neither in the beginning nor in the end. One day in a whole lifetime! But it is a lie. It is a total lie. It was a matter of moments. Just a few moments! The mind was cold. The water was cold. And her bare body was so lovely when the lightning flashed. What is action? What is a man's duty? Where lies responsibility? In action or in no action? How slippery is the moss on a boat? Have you ever tied yourself to a boat with a sari?

"Ah! You are thinking. You think I have lost my balance. I can switch on a light and I can put if off. But there is no electricity, is that my fault? But the moss was so slippery. Moss is God's work. What is man's responsibility? In taking action? But what action did I take? What should I have done? Look! I am perfectly normal. I can switch on the light and switch it off. It is not my fault if there is no electricity. What a flash of lightning there was when she came up the first time. But lightning does not strike the depths of water. Have you ever gone under water? Have you ever taken a dive? Ah! You are thinking! You think I cannot switch on and turn off the light. Wait! I will show you."

For a long time I watched him turning the switches on and off. When we reached my destination, the morning sun had filled the compartment. He lay on the berth with his head between his hands. Getting down from the compartment, I was unable to decide what I could do for him.

★★★

About the Author

Sharat Kumar graduated from the National Defence Academy and was commissioned in the Indian Navy. After nine years of service, including spending a year on deputation to command a company of the Border Roads in North Sikkim, he resigned his commission and joined a private sector industry in Kolkata. After being the Managing Director of the company, he switched to be the President of a Joint Sector company in Srinagar, Kashmir.

Thereafter, he took a year off to write his first novel *Shikhar aur Seemayen* based on his experiences in Sikkim. This novel won the literary award of the Delhi Hindi Academy. It was translated in English as *Orange Moon* and the hard cover was released by Ramakanta Rath, the President of Sahitya Akademi at that time. A pocket book edition has also been published in USA.

His other Hindi novel *Lal Kothi Alvida* was made into a TV serial and eighty-two half hour episodes of it were telecast at prime time by Doordarshan. Thereafter, he directed a full-length feature film *Duvidha* based on this novel. This art film received Certificates of Special Merit at the International Film Festivals at Strasbourg and Philadelphia, and a Mejor Actriz, Rashi B Award at Festival de Granada, and was screened at Festival du Cinema de Bruxelles. This novel has also been translated and published in English as *Farewell Red Mansion*.

Subsequently, he was the Director of a prestigious MBA school (IMT Ghaziabad) when his book *Mind your Management* won the NTPC-IMA award for the 'Best Management Book of the Year'.

Sharat Kumar lives in New Delhi, and has now decided to devote himself to fictional works. (Contact : 9818507829. 41354034, E-mail: sksharatku40@gmail.com)